Awake
on
Garland Street

by

Laura Strickland

Awake on Garland Street

Cover Art by *Diana Carlile*

The Wild Rose Press, Inc.
PO Box 708
Adams Basin, NY 14410-0708
Visit us at www.thewildrosepress.com

Publishing History
First Fantasy Rose Edition, 2016
Print ISBN 978-1-5092-1103-6
Digital ISBN 978-1-5092-1104-3

Published in the United States of America

She'd been telling herself for days—ever since she learned Brendan O'Rourke had landed back in St. John's—she could cope with seeing him. She'd resolved that she wouldn't avoid her usual haunts on his account, wouldn't change her habits. And now here she stood in Fitzgerald's facing him and wishing she could fall through the floor.

He had no right to look so good—better in fact than he had when they parted in a storm of tears and bitter recriminations eight years ago, a break that had shredded her heart.

She'd put that heart back together in the intervening years—or thought she had. Yet here she stood with it bleeding in her chest.

Because those intervening years had been kind to him, very kind. No longer the boy with whom she fell so wildly in love, he'd become the man she'd foreseen, his long, lanky legs clothed in a pair of faded jeans, shoulders encased in a worn leather jacket that looked soft as butter, his reddish-brown hair—full of wave—tumbling over his brow as it always had. The beard was new, but it became him. The lean cheeks, marked by long dimples when he smiled, remained the same, as did those hazel eyes, bright with intelligence and a spark of devilry, set under level brows.

Oh, heaven help her, she still wanted him. And she couldn't let him see it. She absolutely could not let him see.

Praise for Laura Strickland

"I was so caught up and excited to find out the outcome, but still a part of me didn't want the story to end. The author has a talent for writing and telling a story that is sure to capture readers."

~Ginger, Long and Short Reviews

~*~

"I didn't know if Ms. Strickland would give them a HEA or an HFN with this being a short story but I didn't want to stop reading, and could happily have read this as a longer story if she ever chose to rewrite and expand it."

~Honeysuckle at Long and Short Reviews.

Dedication

To Dianne Cohen,
my "woman on the street" in St. John's,
with gratitude for her research and advice.
Any errors herein are entirely mine.

Chapter One

Brendan O'Rourke broke the last threads of sleep and crawled reluctantly into wakefulness. *Not again.* Three days back at the family home in St. John's, Newfoundland, and he'd yet to get a full night's sleep. He had tried every remedy he could imagine, from a warm soothing shower to watching late-night television—even a tot of whiskey. It always ended with him staring wide-eyed into his dark room at around three in the morning.

With fiddle music in his ears.

He had to admit it was damn fine fiddling, some of the best he'd ever heard. And he should know, being an ace fiddler himself as well as a founding member of the famed St. John's Celtic band Kissin' the Cod.

He corrected himself, frowning. Member of the former band Kissin' the Cod. The band had broken up nearly three weeks ago—just remembering that felt like a hard punch to the gut. Over the last decade, ever since leaving high school, he and the lads had worked hard to build a name. Days of solid promo work and nights spent doing what he loved best in the world—fiddling. Weeks lost in touring and the adoration of crowds. Only to see it all drain away like water down a plug hole.

No wonder he couldn't sleep.

That didn't explain the fiddle music he kept hearing, did it?

The first night, straight off the plane from Chicago and exhausted, he'd thought he hallucinated the lilting strains. The second night he blamed it on a dream, but dreams didn't keep running after you woke up, so he'd made a right fool of himself the next day, going 'round to ask the neighbors to keep the music down.

Imagine him telling anyone to turn the volume down after picking up his fiddle at sixteen and never looking back. Anyway, the neighbors hadn't been responsible, even though these old jelly-bean row houses of St. John's were notorious for failing to prevent sound from traveling through the partitioning walls.

The Kennedys on one side had looked at him like he must be crazy or drunk. Old Mrs. Taylor on the other side had dragged him in and fed him a full breakfast, all while reminding him his parents' home, in which he stayed while they were away, was haunted.

He knew that. He'd been born in this house—in his parents' room right across the hall from where he now lay—and had grown up here. Many of the old homes in St. John's claimed resident spirits. As far as he knew, none of the ghosts fiddled like a house afire.

Don't be a fool, he chastened himself as he involuntarily counted the flawless beats in the reel that now filled his ears. This must be the product of the break-up and an overwrought mind.

His imagination, sure.

But he recognized the tune that now echoed through the quiet house—"The Silver Spear." He'd played it countless times with the band, though he had to admit, not like this.

He knew fiddlers, and he knew fiddling. This

musician had a touch similar to his own. Irish-style fiddling, yes, which being an O'Rourke he also favored. But for all its blinding skill, this hovered on the edge of sharp and made a wild dance. Even lying on his back in the bed, Brendan couldn't keep his foot from tapping.

He could think of only one explanation—somebody lurking downstairs played a trick on him. Pretty unlikely, since he was supposed to be alone in the place, house sitting. But he supposed someone could have crept in—someone like his former bandmate and one-time friend, Johnny Rideout, intent on driving him completely out of his mind.

Anger got him out of bed at that thought. He switched on the light, and it showed him the familiar room which his mother must have redecorated after he left home. Narrow and high-ceilinged, the walls shone jewel-tone red, the drapes old gold.

His bare toes dug into the plush area carpet of matching hues. What had his ma been thinking? His room had always been blue and white. Of course, after being away all of eight years, he supposed he could no longer call this his room.

The music that played in his ear—or in his head—switched to a slip jig and, as he hauled open the bedroom door, promptly increased in volume.

Damn it, somebody had actually broken into his family home—for which he was responsible while his parents celebrated their thirtieth anniversary with a summer-long vacation in Europe. Full of indignation and clad only in a pair of plaid boxers, he followed the sound of fiddling out of his room and along the narrow hallway to the top of the stairs. Yes, it came from down there, all right. And if he caught the miscreant, he meant to take him apart with his bare hands.

As soon as he started down the stairs, the rhythm of the music changed again, slowed and glided into a tender, lyrical tune dripping with emotion, enough to touch even Brendan's enraged heart.

Whoever this devil might be, by God he could play the fiddle! Maybe, Brendan reflected as he charged down, he wouldn't break the fellow's fingers—just the rest of him.

From the foot of the stairs, he could tell the music issued from the kitchen at the back of the house. He started down the passageway only to come face to face with a figure standing at the end of the shadowy hall.

He stopped abruptly and stared. Ah, surely he knew that fella? Tall and lanky, with a crop of wild, reddish-brown hair, a lean Irish face, and a luxuriant red beard. Brendan stared into the man's eyes a full moment before breath flooded his lungs. That was him—surely he'd caught his own reflection in a mirror hanging on the far wall.

Then, like a blow to the chest, it hit him: the figure, fully clothed in a soft shirt and rough-woven trousers, had a fiddle in his hand. And no mirror hung at the end of the hallway.

He swore softly and stared harder, blood draining from his face.

At the same moment, an explosive volley of knocking erupted on the front door behind him.

The image at the end of the hall disappeared with an almost audible pop.

Brendan swore again, whirled, and hurried to the front door, which sounded like it was about to be knocked from its hinges. He hauled it open to see Gord

Kennedy, his parents' next-door neighbor, clad only in pajamas and with his hair standing out around his head.

"Not funny!" Kennedy cried.

"Eh?" Brendan had to force the word, most of his attention still centered behind him.

"A man needs his sleep. And to tell you the truth, Doris and I were engaged in something other than sleeping. It's not often I get a leg over these days, b'y. And you have to go interrupt it by playing your fiddle…"

"You heard that?"

"Heard it? The way these houses are built, you could hear a fart in a thunderstorm."

Brendan tipped his head. "Yet when I asked you about it yesterday, you never said you'd heard anything."

Gord scowled. "Didn't want to be rude—Doris said we shouldn't complain. We knows you're a fiddler. Anyways, once I'm asleep I'm asleep. In this case, I just happened to be…"

"I see." Brendan didn't want to think about Gord and Doris—contemporaries of his parents—getting up to nocturnal shenanigans. "Wasn't me playing, Gord."

"What?"

"Wasn't me, I swear. It woke me up too."

Gord paled visibly even in the poor light and crossed himself. "Jesus, Mary, and Joseph. It must be him."

"Who?"

"Your great-grandfather, b'y. Charlie O'Rourke."

"Don't be an idiot. Are you trying to tell me—?"

"A ghost. I believe your parents thought he was gone."

"You're talking nonsense."

"I'm not. Don't you remember? He used to hang about when you were small. This was his house, you know, back in the day. Your ma said you used to talk to him when you were just a sprog."

A chill chased down Brendan's spine, one not caused by the cool night air. "Horse hockey."

Gord shrugged. "Say what you will. But Charlie O'Rourke was a fiddler—a damn fine one." He leaned closer. "Almost as good as you."

Brendan reached out and seized Gord by the front of his pajama shirt. "Are you having me on? Trying to drive me crazy? It's you, isn't it? Playing some recording and trying to convince me it's a ghost. Did Johnny Rideout put you up to it?"

Gord pulled away and brushed himself off indignantly. "Seems likely you're already crazy. Anyway, why should I do such a thing? I don't do Johnny Rideout's bidding."

"Mrs. Taylor never said she heard anything."

"Martha Taylor's deaf as a post. Now, if you'll excuse me, I'll get back to bed while Doris is still halfway in the mood. You shut that ghost up, b'y. Or if you can't shut him up, ask him to stick to playing something romantic like that last tune, at least for the next five minutes or so."

Gord stalked away. Brendan shut the door and leaned against it.

Five minutes? Doris was a lucky woman. But Gord had to be raving. A ghost? The ghost of his great-grandfather Charlie, no less.

Brendan knew about him, sure. Charlie O'Rourke was a legend among members of the family and also the black sheep, if he could be both. He'd been a fiddler like Brendan, true—supposedly one of the first water. He'd also been a reprobate and a drunkard who'd left his wife, Bridget, to pretty much raise their son— Brendan's grandfather—on her own while Charlie flitted around St. John's playing at his music and chatting up other women.

Did Brendan recall encountering him in ghost form while young? Most assuredly not, though he did recall most other details of growing up here. Of course, if he'd been under the age of five or so, he just might not remember.

Which meant it might be true. But nah, it couldn't be. Such things just didn't happen in the twenty-first century.

Even in St. John's.

Chapter Two

"Put another one in here." Brendan tapped his glass, which held only dregs of rich, black ale and a few flecks of foam, and winked at the female bartender. Best ale in North America, here in St. John's. And he should know. He and the band had played all over Canada and the States. Nothing tasted like the brew here at Fitzgerald's.

His best friend from childhood, Barry Tate, leaned on the bar next to him and peered into his eyes. Barry had an honest moonface so homely women tended to fall for it, and fair hair that curled around his ears. He worked conducting tours all around the Avalon Peninsula and claimed he had to drink away the effects afterward.

Now he frowned prodigiously. "Brendan, buddy, pal, old b'y—don't you think you've had enough?"

"Not by half. Barry, I've been wishing for a taste of this ale for the last eight years. Now I'm back home, I'm sure as hell going to enjoy it." He smiled at the approaching bartender and tipped his glass. "Right there, darling."

The bartender complied with a smile of her own and moved off. Barry stared after her pensively. "Think she'd sleep with me?"

Brendan almost choked on his ale. Barry had been asking that same, plaintive question since they were both sixteen. Some things never changed.

God, it felt good to be home.

He too eyed the bartender, a pretty little redhead. "Maybe." Barry had surprising success with women, which made Brendan wonder why the man remained so morose about his chances.

He lowered his voice and confided to his friend, "I need to drink a skinful so I can go home and sleep tonight."

Barry gave him a surprised stare. "You having trouble sleeping? Since when? You could always fall asleep in the blink of an eye. Remember that time in biology class when you were sound asleep and old man Roberts called on you? You woke up, thought you were in history class and began sounding off about the First World War."

"Old man Roberts always detested me."

Barry snorted. "Said you'd never amount to anything. He should see you now. How many millions have you made?"

"No millions, b'y." But many, many thousands.

"And all those women fawning at your feet."

There had been some fawning. Astonishing how eager girls were to sleep with a Celtic fiddle player.

"Band's gone bust now," he said unhappily. "All that's done."

"Ah, nah—" Barry dismissed it with a shrug and leaned on the bar. "You'll get back together, sure. Nobody'd be thick enough to throw away that kind of success."

"Johnny Rideout's thick enough."

Barry shrugged. He knew Johnny and the other members of Kissin' the Cod well. They'd all grown up together and understood each other's flaws and strong points.

"So why did you fall out?"

Brendan grunted. "A woman. No, not like you think. Johnny started seeing someone steady in Chicago. He let it interfere with the band."

"How so?"

"Spent all kinds of time with her, began missing practice and a few recording sessions—was even late to a performance. So we had it out. I told him we've all had to make sacrifices." God knew he, Brendan, had. "Told him this woman—Chrissy—would have to come second. He announced she was pregnant with his kid, so it would have to be the band that came second. We had a big blow-up and I haven't talked to him since."

That had surprised Brendan. He'd been sure Johnny would come crawling back, admit he was wrong to toss away all their hard work and their dreams for the future. Over a damned woman.

Brendan knew for a fact women were thick on the ground. He also knew he'd long ago done exactly what he expected Johnny to do now.

He took a mouthful of ale and grimaced. "I've talked to Ned and Rory." The other band members. "They've talked to Johnny. He and I…"

It inflicted hurt deeper than Brendan had expected. He'd come home to watch his parents' house, lick his wounds, and let Johnny realize his mistake. Which Johnny had failed to do as yet. "Johnny can be stubborn," he concluded, closing the subject.

"He can, he can, b'y. But not a patch on you. You've got a head of solid rock."

"Me?"

"If you didn't, you couldn't put away as much ale as you do and still manage to play the fiddle. So is that why you're having trouble sleeping? The fall-out with Johnny?"

"No."

"What is it, then?"

"You wouldn't believe me if I told you."

"Try me." Barry signaled the bartender for still another refill.

Brendan lowered his voice to a spectral level. "There's a ghost in our house."

"Sure." Barry glanced at him. "The ghost of Charlie O'Rourke. Everybody knows that."

Brendan stared. "Oh, yes?"

"Yes, b'y. Your great-grandfather, wasn't he? And a worse reprobate than yourself."

"I'm no—"

"Spent his life drunk and fiddling, so they say. Took time only to sire your grandfather and died in shame. But oh, the talent! Passed that straight down to you, so it seems."

"Died in shame?" Brendan's parents had never mentioned that.

Barry gave the bartender a hangdog look as she refilled his glass, and went on, "In fact, you know the ghost tour?"

"Yes." A guide led visitors around the city at night, talking up the haunted places.

"Organizers have been trying for years to get that house on the roster. Your mom's dead set against it."

"Thank God." Brendan could think of few things worse than peering out the front windows and seeing a crowd of gawkers.

11

"So, Charlie O'Rourke's keeping you awake, eh?"

"I don't want to talk about it." And suddenly Brendan didn't. He had to go back to that house when he left the bar. He hastily fished for another topic and inadvertently chose the last one he should.

"How's Mary Grace?"

"Well, b'y, as for that—"

"Did I hear my name?"

The query came from behind them and spun both men around. For the second time in as many days Brendan felt like he'd been punched in the gut. Because there she stood—large as life and twice as beautiful.

He'd promised himself he could guard against this, when he decided to come home. St. John's wasn't so big he could avoid bumping into her forever. But with her safely married, he'd believed he could handle it.

God, had he been wrong.

Emotions closed his throat, and he had to clear it twice before he could speak. "Hello, Mary Grace."

She sported a pair of tight-fitting black pants that caressed her slim figure and an oversized shirt that had slid aside to reveal one shoulder. Her long hair, worn loose, fell down her back in glossy brown waves. And her eyes, blue-gray and fringed by those incredible, long lashes, met his with a measure of defiance. Or was that hurt?

He tried to look away from her eyes and found he couldn't. Instead he fell, tumbled helplessly into a vortex of ale fumes, regret, and instantaneous lust.

A smile, not particularly pleasant, curved her lips. Brendan had kissed those lips—and that shoulder too— more times than he could now count. He'd kissed her everywhere.

And wanted to again.

"Brendan O'Rourke, as I live and breathe. I heard a rumor you were back in town, but I didn't quite believe it. As soon as you spoke my name, though, I knew the worst. Nobody but you ever calls me 'Mary Grace.' "

"Grace," he hastily corrected himself. She liked to go by her middle name. But he'd whispered that other into her ear at such searing, tantalizing moments...

She measured him up and down with a glance. "Still just the same, I see. Supping ale and propping up the bar." She widened her eyes in mock surprise. "Ah, but where's your fiddle? The one to which you wed yourself, I mean. Never say you left her home alone."

Dismay soured Brendan's stomach. For an instant he thought he'd lose all the lovely ale he'd just consumed. He choked it back manfully and turned the question around. "How's Chet—your husband?" Last he'd heard, Mary Grace had been planning her wedding to Chet Hader, a stuffed shirt of the first water who'd incidentally been head of his class in school and now earned a fortune investing in real estate.

At Brendan's side, Barry moved spasmodically.

Mary Grace's gaze flicked to Barry and back to Brendan. She tossed her head.

"I see Loose Lips, here, hasn't got 'round to telling you."

" 'Loose Lips'?" Barry echoed indignantly.

She shot him another scathing look. "You know you couldn't keep a secret if your life depended on it, Barry Tate."

"It's no secret," Barry said. To Brendan he added, "She broke up with Hader just before the wedding. Virtually left him standing at the altar."

Chapter Three

How unfair could life be? Grace Dawe bit the inside of her lip so hard it brought tears to her eyes. She'd been telling herself for days—ever since she learned Brendan O'Rourke had landed back in St. John's—she could cope with seeing him. She'd resolved that she wouldn't avoid her usual haunts on his account, wouldn't change her habits. And now here she stood in Fitzgerald's facing him and wishing she could fall through the floor.

He had no right to look so good—better in fact than he had when they parted in a storm of tears and bitter recriminations eight years ago, a break that had shredded her heart.

She'd put that heart back together in the intervening years—or thought she had. Yet here she stood with it bleeding in her chest.

Because those intervening years had been kind to him, very kind. No longer the boy with whom she fell so wildly in love, he'd become the man she'd foreseen, his long, lanky legs clothed in a pair of faded jeans, shoulders encased in a worn leather jacket that looked soft as butter, his reddish-brown hair—full of wave— tumbling over his brow as it always had. The beard was new, but it became him. The lean cheeks, marked by long dimples when he smiled, remained the same, as did those hazel eyes, bright with intelligence and a spark of devilry, set under level brows.

Oh, heaven help her, she still wanted him. And she couldn't let him see it. She absolutely could not let him see.

She sought desperately for something to say.

Brendan spoke before she could. "Is that true?"

Oh, and that voice—warm and deep, flavored by the accent he hadn't lost in all his time away. She remembered that all too well vibrating in her ear, heating her blood, skittering across her soul.

"Not quite. I broke it off the night before. We'd not yet reached the church."

"Nobody told me."

His eyes hadn't flickered from hers, and his regard did strange things to her insides. She tried to free herself from his gaze and failed.

"Why should anybody think to tell you, Brendan O'Rourke? You were busy dashing around the world. And," she added deliberately, "it's not as if it mattered to you, whether or not I got married."

He flushed. She couldn't tell whether it was with anger or some other emotion. He broke eye contact with her at last and took a long draught of ale.

"You're right."

Grace reeled. She felt like she'd been struck in the face.

Again.

She didn't need this. She didn't need *him*. She had to walk away.

She wasn't sure she could.

"So," she said to fill the terrible silence, "how long are you—?"

"So," he spoke at the same moment, "why did you

break it off?"

"That's a personal question."

Another silence fell, this one edged with briars. This is why we broke up, Grace thought. Because he's impossible. Because he's bad for me, because I had a moment of sanity eight years ago that let me see those truths.

Then why couldn't she walk away? How did he hold her here against her will, her thoughts drawn to that body beneath his clothes and how his hands could play a fiddle—or a woman?

Barry, being Barry, horned in. "Brendan and I were just speaking about his house being haunted."

Brendan shot him a look of annoyance. Willing to seize on anything that might distract her from the unwelcome feelings streaming through her, Grace took it up. "Afraid of a ghost are you, Brendan O'Rourke? And isn't it supposed to be some relation of yours?"

"Great-grandfather." He supped more ale, again with his eyes on her. "And I'm not afraid of him, quite. It's just fecking annoying when he starts fiddling in the middle of the night. I've had no sleep."

"Never heard of him fiddling," Barry said. "Just appearing to folks, usually falling-down drunk."

Grace snorted. "Figures."

Brendan drew himself up. "I am not drunk," he pronounced with an insistence that argued he might be well on his way.

Why am I wasting my time here? He hasn't changed. Still the wild-hearted, talented dreamer. Still the good-time lad.

Still irresistible.

"Anyway," he went on, "I shouldn't think you'd

believe in ghosts. You're far too practical. A *realist*."

Ah, so he did remember. But how dared he throw it back in her face, the word she'd hurled at him when they parted for the last time?

Be a realist, Brendan. Will you throw away all we have together for some mad dream of making it with the band? Because if you go now, that's what you're doing—throwing me away.

He'd gone anyway, damn him. And double damn him because he and the band had made it big after all.

She shrugged, feigning carelessness. "I'm Irish, aren't I?"

"Irish and English," he said darkly. "No telling what that stubborn English streak will make you do."

"I don't need this." She said it aloud this time. "Nice seeing you, but I'm gone." She'd walk out on him this time. See how he liked it.

"No, stay," Barry bleated. "Let me buy you a drink."

They both stared at him.

"Honestly?" Grace said. "You're hitting on me?"

"Well, you're single now, right? Available."

"I may be single; that doesn't make me available. I've outgrown my foolish need for still more foolish men."

"I understand they do make appliances." Barry pulled a droll face. "But I don't expect they're as good as warm flesh and blood. On the other hand," he reflected, "probably have to be better than Chet Hader."

Brendan grinned, that old, crooked, devil-may-care grin that used to turn Grace's blood to lava.

She found it still did.

So he thought that funny, did he? Immature dolt.

"Don't be an arsehole," she told Barry. "In case you didn't notice, I already have a drink. I'm perfectly capable of buying myself drinks. I don't need to bat my eyelashes and get free ones."

"Ah, darling." Barry leaned toward her. "Bat them for me anyway—do."

Brendan laughed, and the sound went through Grace, knocked her back a number of years to when they'd been together, really together, bone and blood, when she'd believed nothing could ever part them.

She recoiled as if she'd been slapped. Fortunately, the two men probably thought she withdrew from Barry's leering face.

She spoke a word no lady should utter, tossed back the last of her ale, and slammed her glass on the bar. Whirling on her heel, she marched out with all the dignity she could muster.

Ah hell, she thought bitterly, and here she'd thought—hoped—maybe she was over the man.

****

Still at the bar, Brendan stared into his glass, his appetite for ale all at once flown. He felt as if he'd just been reamed out by a chainsaw, and it bothered him more than it should.

"An ugly encounter, and no mistake," said Barry, putting it into words. "That girl always did have a tongue that could flay you alive—and do a lot of other things if I can believe what you said back then."

"Don't remind me." Brendan groaned. But Barry didn't need to remind him; the memories came flooding unbidden: the first time he and Mary Grace had been together up in that same room where he now spent his nights sleepless, half listening for his folks to come home—at least until she'd applied that tongue and blasted all his brain cells to oblivion; the last time they'd been together, not knowing the very next day would see them part for good, and the depth of their passion.

How could he have thrown that away?

How could he have done anything else? Even now he had no answer.

"You think her vow of celibacy will hold?" Barry asked. "Pitiful shame, a beautiful, lovely girl like that."

"Maybe." Brendan knew—had encountered—the iron will that lay beneath Mary Grace's beauty. "Where's she working now? Still at the museum?" When he left she'd been employed out on Cape Spear at the reproduction outport village.

Barry cocked an eye at him. "You haven't heard? She's in charge of the place now and doing a damned fine job. They've expanded out there and offer extended visits where people can get a true taste of life in 1800. They've been written up in every guidebook in existence, and they're a regular stop on our Cape Spear tour."

"Good for her," Brendan said and meant it.

"Yes, b'y, and you should see her all dressed up in her nineteenth-century garb. It's a sight for sore eyes, so I assure you."

Probably better if Brendan didn't see it.

"But you know," Barry mused on, "I suppose she had to put her energies somewhere. She with the museum, you with your music." In a gesture that echoed Mary Grace's parting one, Barry drained his glass. "Truth is, though, if I were a betting man—"

"You are a betting man. 'Any vice going,' you

always say."

"Yes, b'y, and sometimes more than one a night." Barry winked. "But as I was saying, had I put money on it, I'd never have expected the two of you to break up, not even given all the arguments. You were too...too..."

"Solid?"

"I was going to say too much in love." Barry clapped Brendan on the shoulder. "But now I suppose you've had women—groupies—all 'round the country. So you knew what you were doing after all."

"Groupies, is it?"

"Scads of women."

"They come 'round. You'd be surprised how seldom I've taken advantage." And not one of them had measured up to Mary Grace Dawe. And just maybe, Brendan reflected, that explained why there had been so few.

Chapter Four

The minute his head hit the pillow, Brendan knew he had no hope of sleeping despite all the good ale he'd consumed. This time, though, thoughts of Mary Grace rather than fiddle music kept him awake.

He tossed and turned for more than an hour, thinking about everything from the way Mary Grace's hair used to smell to the silken feel of her skin beneath his lips, before his ensuing condition got him back up out of bed, brain buzzing and groin aching.

Maybe a hot—or cold—shower would do the trick. Maybe another drink. He wondered if his dad still kept a stash of bottles behind the storage boxes on the back porch.

He barreled down the stairs and into the dim kitchen, only to be brought up short so suddenly his bare feet skidded on the floor.

Someone leaned in the doorway that led out back, only dimly illuminated by the ambient light from outside.

Eyes locked on the figure, Brendan reached out and flipped on the kitchen light. The figure promptly faded.

"Works better with the light off." The voice sounded low and rough, with a rich Newfoundland accent.

Brendan flipped the switch back off and stared. "Who in hell are you?"

"A foolish question. For one thing, lad, I'm not in Hell, at least not yet. For another, do I really need to tell you who I am?"

A chill drenched Brendan from his head downward, relieving him of all necessity for that cold shower. "Uh—"

"Never thought I'd need to convince my own flesh and blood of my identity. Now, lad, I could not claim to be the smartest man in St. John's. But from the look of you standing there gawping, I fear the brain power of the O'Rourkes has sadly drained away."

"You're Grandfather Charlie."

"Great-grandfather to you. And yes, it's Charlie O'Rourke, at your service." The ghost—for Brendan could no longer deny the evidence before him—sketched a bow and tottered where he stood.

"You look like me."

The ghost glanced down at himself. "I suppose I do, at that. Clothing's different, of course, me being dressed properly and you wearing almost nothing. Other than that, I'd say there's a fair resemblance."

"Resemblance? The first time I saw you I thought I was looking in a mirror."

"I imagine the blood breeds true. I'm the better looking of us two, of course."

"You think so?"

"I regret to say, Grandson, I do. Apart from that, you and I are more alike than you'd think. Truth to tell, that's why I've come."

"You've been playing fiddle music in the middle of the night."

The ghost's expression brightened. "So you heard me?"

"Heard you? I've barely had a wink of sleep. The neighbors heard you also and thought it was me."

"Never mind the neighbors." Charlie waved a hand. "'Tis your attention I wanted to grab."

"Well, damn, you've got it. Now can I get some sleep?"

"Not so fast, lad. You sit yourself down there at that table. We're going to have a serious conversation."

"Talk? You want to talk?"

"I do. I come with a message from beyond the grave." Charlie leaned forward, leered, and stumbled.

Brendan narrowed his eyes. "You're drunk."

"What's that, lad? What d'you say?"

"Stinking, falling-down drunk. How can that be? You're dead."

"Well, you see, it's all down to a little thing called whiskey. Water of life, it is, and—as it turns out—of death."

"But you're a ghost. Ghosts can't drink."

"Can they not?" Charlie widened eyes all too much like Brendan's and feigned astonishment. "I must have one hell of a buzz on, then. It's lasted almost seventy years."

"Is that how long you've been dead?"

"Yes, lad, and I had a skinful when I went down that night." He appeared to reflect. "I had a skinful most times, back then."

Brendan blinked, trying desperately to reconcile what he saw—and heard. Maybe he'd fallen asleep upstairs after all. Yes, that had to be it This mad scene must be a dream produced by the ale. How else would he come up with an intoxicated ghost?

"Sit down," the ghost ordered.

23

"I don't think—"

"That was not a request!" The ghost barked. The chair nearest Brendan slid out from the table under its own power—or maybe under Charlie's power.

Brendan stared at it. "You can do that?"

Charlie looked smug. "I can do a lot of things. I can open and shut doors, float through walls, make objects hover in the air." He waved nimble fingers as if casting a spell. "All manner of spooky shenanigans. So I suggest you sit down there before I knock you on your arse."

Brendan snorted, but he sat. Charlie moved to a chair on the opposite side of the table, weaving like a sot on a bender, and tumbled into it.

That rather ruined the effect when he said, "I'll have you remember, Brendan Patrick O'Rourke, you're still my great-grandson, and as such you owe me a show of respect."

"You've kept me awake for three nights, you're falling-down drunk—and dead—yet I'm supposed to show you respect?"

"As is due your elders. I know your ma raised you better than to be disrespectful. A good woman is your mother, lad. My grandson did well marrying her, and he's done right by her, as I'm happy to say."

"You came from beyond the grave and sat me down in the dark kitchen to talk about my ma?"

"No, you foolish dolt. To talk about women in general."

"Women." Definitely a dream—no doubt the effect of seeing Mary Grace again after so long.

"I was married, you know, when I died."

"Well, yes, I figure…"

"Close your trap when I'm after telling you something. My wife, Bridget, she was a good woman as well—faultless and beautiful. A star in the heavens."

Brendan stole a glance at the clock on the wall. Yep, even by the dim light he could see the second hand moving.

God, this must be real. Heaven help him.

He resisted the impulse to cross himself, which he hadn't done since he was about eight years old.

"I'm glad you had a good wife, Grandfather. But what has that to do with—?"

"You've a decided tendency to flap your gums, do you know that? Be quiet when a person's relating something."

"Technically, you're not a person."

" 'Technically'?"

"Your *personhood*, more or less, is lying in a graveyard somewhere."

"Don't remind me. I died at the ripe old age of thirty-two. Thirty-two, lad! What do you think of that? Threw my future away and left my matchless Bridget to struggle on alone and raise our wee son." The ghost cut Brendan a look. "You can't be far off from that age yourself."

"I've a few years yet."

"Then you still have time." Charlie leaned forward. In the ambient light that filtered into the kitchen, Brendan could both see him *and see through him*, which turned his stomach a bit queasy.

"Take a warning by me," the ghost intoned. "Do not make the mistakes I made. For, lad, I can see you're headed down the same road I took. And you don't want to end up like me, do you?"

Brendan thought about it: drunk, transparent, a pain in the arse to his descendants. On the other hand, Charlie still played the fiddle. Brendan decided that didn't make up for spending eternity intoxicated, and he shook his head violently.

"Very wise. Then you'll need to place yourself in my hands. Submit to my guidance. This here will be but the first of many sessions we'll have while you're in the family homestead. I figure we can meet here each night till I whip your character into shape."

"Look, Grandfather, with all due respect, I'm going to need my sleep. This has to stop. And there's absolutely nothing wrong with my character."

"Is there not? Tell me, Grandson, what's the most powerful force on earth?"

Brendan didn't even have to think about it. "Music."

"That's what I used to suppose. But you're wrong. The most powerful force in the whole universe is *love*."

This time Brendan's snort didn't even approach polite. "I'm not sitting here listening to this clap-trap." He pushed to his feet. "I'm off to bed. And I suggest you let me sleep this time, old man."

Charlie arose also, swaying a bit. "Bah—talking to you is like lecturing a twelve-week-old infant. Off to your bed then, wee one. Just so you know, we're not done. We won't be done till I make you see the error of my ways. And," Charlie added morosely, "hopefully attain my redemption."

Chapter Five

Grace leveled her gaze on the sunrise and threw back her head, drawing in a deep breath of salt air. To her, a sunrise at Cape Spear surpassed any in the world. And she'd seen her share of sunrises—in Paris, at Stonehenge, Rio de Janiero, even Siberia. The year after Brendan O'Rourke broke her heart—damn him— she'd been such a mess she just had to get away from St. John's. She'd left her budding job at the museum, tossed away her other responsibilities, taken her inheritance from her grandmother Coates, and tramped the world with a backpack on her shoulders and pain in her heart.

In the end, though, she'd had to come back to St. John's—cured, she hoped—because home was home, and the place flowed through her blood.

Standing here on the spear of land that reached like a finger toward Ireland—the easternmost point on the continent, in fact—with ocean all around her and waves crashing on the rocks below the observation deck, only one question possessed her mind.

Was Brendan O'Rourke in her blood as well?

Last week she'd have said no, would have bet her life she'd beaten the infatuation and won her way free after eight years and a love affair with another man, if what she'd had with Chet could be called that. Then she'd walked into Fitzgerald's, seen Brendan standing there propping up the bar, and tumbled harder than if she'd leaped onto those rocks below.

She couldn't understand it. She'd known handsomer men. Hell, she'd dated handsomer men than Brendan O'Rourke. Something about him just tripped her wire. Always had.

Always would?

No, no, no. She wouldn't allow that, refused to let him take her heart in his hands and shred it again.

She needed to use his reappearance here in St. John's as a lesson, a message to herself that she'd passed far beyond the bounds of needing a man, any man. Even Brendan.

"What I need," she whispered to the holy sunrise, "is a new beginning. Bring me one, please."

The new sun stared back at her like a baleful eye—or perhaps a benevolent one. Hard to tell. All in your perspective, maybe.

She turned her back on the ocean and tramped back up the board walkway, past the lighthouse to the parking area where her car waited. Several other vehicles kept hers company at this hour, the sunrise at Cape Spear being a favorite with tourists.

Grace climbed into her car and blew out a breath. She wondered just how long Brendan O'Rourke intended to stay in St. John's. Not long, she hoped. For the foreseeable future she'd better avoid his haunts if she could, though the very idea of doing so irritated her. No more stops at Fitzgerald's or the other bars along George Street where he might drink and play music.

Oh, lord, she definitely wasn't ready to listen to him play that fiddle of his. Because it might well unravel the last of her resistance.

The first time they'd made love—and yes, it had been *love* even back then, at least on her part—was after he'd played that damned fiddle for her and her alone. A slow and sensual rendition of "The Star of the County Down," if she recalled correctly. And she did. She'd been seventeen and he eighteen; she'd never been with anyone before him.

When he'd laid that fiddle aside and begun to touch her instead, she'd been lost body and soul.

Yes, but, she lectured herself sternly now, you were a girl then. You believed in mad things like love.

Now she knew better. She had no need for foolish games of the heart. Or selfish men. And Brendan O'Rourke was selfish as they came.

"I'm not wasting any more time on that long drink of water," she said aloud, and started the car.

She drove back up the Spear to the museum, knowing she'd arrive early; she frequently did. Sometimes she slept there, which made the pilgrimage to Cape Spear easier. The museum didn't open till ten a.m., and the lot stood empty when she arrived. Fine with her—she liked it when the replica outport stood empty, the stages catching the morning sunshine and the saltbox houses scattered across the rock like jewels. She parked out of the way and headed for her office in the administration building, also housed in a weathered saltbox.

No new paint here, and precious few luxuries, but Cabot, the resident Newfoundland dog, awaited her with his panting smile. She ruffled his fur, thinking how in truth just feeding such an animal would have been a luxury in the typical outport. Life there had been hard. She should know. Her own ancestors had come from

Kelligrews.

Cabot followed her inside, where she gave him his breakfast and settled down to catch up on paperwork before the regular museum employees arrived, everyone in costume just like hers.

Her office clerk, Darcy Butler, breezed in right before opening time. She glanced at Grace and did a double take.

"Well, now, you're in early again, and up to your eyebrows, from the look of it."

"Going to be a busy day. We have not one but two school tours coming through, and I know I'll be on point later."

"Doesn't mean you need to wear yourself to the bone." Darcy paused with a hand on one generous hip. With her buxom build and blonde hair that refused to stay confined to a bun, she looked more tavern wench than office employee. "You could delegate a bit."

"I do delegate. Don't know what I'd do without you."

"I suppose you slept here again last night."

"No, I was home, not that you could call it sleep." Grace rubbed fitfully at her forehead, where pain lodged.

There were certain advantages to being curator— she had the keys to all the houses, and she loved the way this place felt when everyone had gone, loved her berth upstairs in the house closest to the shore and the heartbeat of the waves all night long.

"Let me get you a cup of tea, and you can tell me what's up."

"Up? What makes you think anything's up?"

Darcy plugged in the electric kettle before she

replied, "The look of you, for one thing. I'm guessing it's a man."

Grace said nothing. Darcy came and nudged out a chair beside Grace's desk before she said, "Tell me it's not Chet again. He's not still trying to talk you into getting back with him?"

"No. Thank God." Grace rested her head in her hands. You'd think he could take a hint. Getting virtually left at the altar would be enough to dissuade some men. Not Chet Hader who, convinced they could get to the bottom of whatever bothered Grace about the idea of marriage, haunted her like—well, like a ghost.

The trouble was, she suspected what bothered her about the idea of marriage had just returned to St. John's. Big as life and twice as attractive.

"Someone new?" Darcy brightened. She had a poorly concealed conviction that Grace need only find the right man in order to mend her world.

Grace knew better. No more men for her. Not ever.

She looked into her friend's eyes. "More like, I met somebody *old*."

It took Darcy a moment to grasp her meaning. "You mean someone from your past? Who?"

Darcy had never known Brendan O'Rourke—she'd been about thirteen back in the day. And Grace rarely talked about her past. She didn't want to know.

"Just someone I used to date. I bumped into him by accident yesterday evening. It came as a bit of a shock."

Darcy bustled off to make the tea and returned with two cups. "Oh, I hate it when that happens. You always wind up looking at him and wondering, what did I see in that?"

"Well, not quite."

"So how long ago did you date him?"

"Eight years."

"Who broke it off—him or you?"

A good question. Grace contemplated it while continuing to massage her forehead. "I guess you could say it was mutual. He made a choice, and I couldn't live with it."

Darcy's big, blue eyes widened. "He chose another woman?"

"No—music." Grace's lips twisted. "You may have heard of Brendan O'Rourke."

Darcy gaped. "From Kissin' the Cod? You dated him? God, he's hot."

Wasn't he, just. "I'm sure a million girls around the country think so."

"I heard a rumor the band broke up—creative differences."

"I expect that's why he's come home."

"Awkward," Darcy conceded. "Especially if you still have feelings for him." She lowered her voice. "Do you?"

That question had kept Grace awake most the night. She had feelings, all right: anger, hurt, betrayal. She shouldn't give the man that kind of power over her.

"Of course not."

"Do you think he'll do the round of the bars and play while he's here? I'd love to hear him. And I'd love to get his autograph if I can."

"If I know Brendan O'Rourke, he won't stray far from his fiddle. After all, it's his mistress."

****

"So I was hoping, Brendan, lad, you'd do the honor of playing at our fundraiser," Father Hurley said humbly. "It's this Sunday. Short notice, I know, but it would only be a couple of tunes, and I know the folks would love to hear you."

Brendan eyed the priest who—frail, white-haired, and full of energy—barely reached his ear. They'd encountered each other on a street corner while Brendan tried to walk off last night's funk.

"Well, Father," he began. Hard to say no. The man had christened him and bullied him for years in religious studies. "It's this way. I've come home with the intention of lying low. No public appearances."

Father Hurley's white eyebrows twitched. "Yes, but I'm willing to bet you've been frequenting the bars, haven't you?"

"Well…"

"And I do not doubt taking your fiddle with you."

"Not yet." Brendan couldn't swear it would never happen. Already his fingers twitched with the desire to play. It started in the very tips and built like longing.

"And if you'll give the sinners in those boozers a tune, why not play to benefit the Church that nurtured you in its bosom? Do you not owe us at least that much? This is one of our best fundraisers of the year, and I know you'll sell a slew of tickets." Father Hurley frowned. "What's the name of your group, now? Something to do with a trout?"

"Kissin' the Cod. But I'm not with the band anymore. We've come apart."

"I'm sorry to hear that. You were quite successful, so I understand."

"Just a bit."

"I hope you get back together. And I'm sure you'll want to keep in form while you're in St. John's."

Brendan, tottering on the brink of defeat, sighed. "Tell you what, Father—I'll do you a deal."

Father Hurley drew himself up. "The Church doesn't do deals, son."

"Maybe in this case you'll make an exception." Brendan leaned closer. "I'd like my parents' house blessed. Holy water, incense—the whole shebang."

Father Hurley looked shocked. "And just why does the O'Rourke house need blessing?" His eyes narrowed abruptly. "Don't tell me it's Charlie O'Rourke again. That old reprobate! I thought he'd settled, for all his sins."

Nonplussed and not sure how to reply, Brendan hemmed and hawed. "I just thought the house could use a bit of a blessing, Father."

"A 'bit of a blessing' with holy water."

"Something like that." Brendan, who now hadn't slept in four nights, could barely think straight. Though Charlie hadn't kept him up last night so much as had memories of Mary Grace.

"Tell you what, son—you scratch my back and I'll scratch yours. I'll be by after Friday Mass with the holy water."

Brendan succumbed. "All right."

"And you get yourself out to the Living Outport Museum this afternoon. Mary Grace Dawe, who runs the place, is making arrangements for the fundraiser."

Brendan's heart hit the ground so hard he expected it to bounce. "You mean it's not at the Church?"

"No, the Museum agreed to let us hold it there this year."

"But Mary Grace Dawe isn't even Catholic."

Father Hurley sniffed. "No—Anglican. But she has

a good heart despite that, and we're raising money for the poor of St. John's, so I trust you'll play your best." Father Hurley lowered his eyebrows. "Given the fact that your grandfather and your great-grandmother Bridget were once among the poor of this city—back when Charlie O'Rourke abandoned them."

Chapter Six

Late afternoon had come and gone before Grace even thought about taking a lunch break. The school tours had completed their rounds in quick succession, followed by a visit from the plumber subsequently called to unblock two toilets in the well-disguised public block.

A coincidence? Grace didn't think so. She paused for a breather at last in her office, where Darcy gamely worked at typing up financial reports due by the end of the day, all too aware she operated on insufficient sleep and nothing more than the cup of tea Darcy had given her earlier.

Suddenly the steady clack of Darcy's keyboard ceased as the clerk looked up and froze.

"Oh. My. Lord."

Darcy, gaping at the door of the office, prompted Grace to whirl. Much like Darcy's fingers, she froze.

Brendan O'Rourke hovered in the doorway— temptation in two boots—tall enough so it seemed his unruly head must brush the top lintel. If he'd looked good in the dusky gloom of Fitzgerald's, he looked ten times better in daylight. Surprise hit Grace first, with desire close on its heels. Anger came to her rescue soon after, and allowed her to speak.

"Will you stop sneaking up on me, Brendan O'Rourke?"

He grinned, damn him—the crooked, rakish grin that had once coaxed Grace to do anything.

"It was you snuck up on me last night, Mary Grace."

"It's Grace. Just Grace. Nobody uses my first name anymore."

He nodded, looking innocent, but said, "And just look at you in that get-up. Good enough to eat."

Grace blushed, something she hadn't done in at least five years. How dared he walk in and act all familiar? On the other hand, he hadn't so much as glanced at Darcy, despite the fact that, generously built, Darcy always threatened to spill from her costume.

"Can I do something for you, O'Rourke?"

He measured her with those clever, hazel eyes that always seemed to carry a spark of light. At one time she'd believed it was a glimpse of his soul. Now she read it for pure devilment.

"Father Hurley sent me, for my sins."

"You certainly have enough of those." Grace had to get a grip. She was letting her waspishness gain the upper hand and losing all professionalism. Surely that was the answer here—acting the professional. "I suppose this is about the fundraiser. Has he persuaded you to play?"

Persuade. Her mind ricocheted to the night he'd persuaded her—with kisses and laughter—up the stairs to his room while his parents were away, when everything had suddenly become serious—the first time they'd made love.

Oh, God. Why did I have to think about that now?

Or the time he'd persuaded her to walk up Signal Hill with him in the dark. They'd watched the moon spread her silver skirt over the ocean and wound up making love there, too.

A persuasive man was Brendan O'Rourke.

"The good Father and I have something of a deal, so yes, I'll be performing. This is the first time I've seen the museum up close. Mary Grace, I'm impressed. And you're in charge of all this?"

He needn't act so surprised. What did he suppose she'd done with these past years of her life while he gallivanted hither and yon? "Thank you. Brendan. This is my clerk, Darcy Butler. My right-hand woman."

Darcy stumbled to her feet and took Brendan's hand. "My goodness, Brendan O'Rourke! I'm a great fan, I assure you. But there's a rumor Kissin' the Cod broke up. Please tell me it's not true."

"No, I'm afraid the rumor is true, Darcy."

"Well, I'm sure it's just temporary."

"Too soon to tell yet. Never hurts to slow things down a beat anyway, clear the head. The band's been working hard and steady, and I'm glad for this chance to come home for a while."

His gaze strayed back to Grace.

Darcy kept talking. "You know, you could always launch a solo career. Musicians do that all the time. And if you don't mind me saying, I've always thought your fiddle made Kissin' the Cod what it was. Such fire!"

"Well, now, that's very kind of you."

"Will you be playing 'round town while you're here? My boyfriend, Billy, plays guitar, and if you like I could have him join you, sit in for a few sessions. I know he'd be pleased—honored, in fact—and you could see how you get on."

"Not sure what I'll get up to while I'm here. But you know anybody's welcome to sit in at places like Fitzgerald's."

"Oh, he'll be thrilled. Playing with Brendan O'Rourke! Meanwhile, could I get your autograph?" Darcy nearly fell over herself snatching up a pen and a piece of paper which Grace couldn't help but notice turned out to be a page from the financial report.

Grace sighed. Sickening. But she had to admit Brendan handled it gracefully and with apparent enjoyment. Well, what man wouldn't enjoy having lovely young girls fawning at his feet?

She waited while the two of them continued to chat for several minutes, watched the light appear and disappear in Brendan's eyes, and began to worry all over again about his effect on her. If she had to deal with him—and it seemed she would—she must find a way to counteract that effect.

Remember how it had felt when he walked out on her, perhaps—yes, that should do it.

When Darcy ran off to get them drinks from the concession by the parking lot, Grace said dryly, "I suppose that happens everywhere you go."

He didn't pretend to misunderstand. He gave an odd shrug that twisted his shoulders, and the bright gaze returned to Grace's face.

"It does. Goes with the territory, I'm afraid." He drew a breath. "It's good to see you, Mary Grace. So good."

Stop calling me that.

She produced a smile she hoped looked polite. "Yes. So how did Father Hurley finagle you into helping at the fundraiser?"

"He's agreed to perform an exorcism at the house."

Grace stared. "You're fooling."

"Not at all. I meant what I said at Fitzgerald's last night. It truly is the ghost of my great-grandfather, Charlie. I've spoken with him. He's on something of a mission."

"Is he!"

"Yes, to reform my character."

"Good luck to him."

"That's what I say. But I've barely slept since I got home, and he has to go. So making a little deal with Father Hurley's no great shakes."

"A word of advice: don't go 'round telling people you're having conversations with the ghost in your house, or they'll decide Kissin' the Cod broke up due to your impending insanity."

"Not necessarily. This is St. John's. Spirits abound, at least according to what Barry says."

"If you begin listening to Barry Tate, I'll start believing you're crazy." Grace shrugged. "But each to his own. What sort of performance did you have in mind?"

He took a long moment before he replied. His bright hazel gaze moved over her again in a way that raised her temperature several degrees. "Don't know. Why don't we meet later to discuss it?"

"Later?"

"Just you and me, at my place."

"You, me, and the ghost?" She'd have to be crazy indeed to agree to any such thing.

"I don't think he'll mind."

"Let's get one thing straight, Brendan. We may have to work together so far as the fundraiser's concerned, but that's where it stops. Understand? I'm not your plaything. And there are plenty of sycophants in this town likely all too ready to fall at your feet."

"Are you suggesting I find some?"

"Yes." No. "That is, I don't care. Just keep out of my way."

He tipped his head in that manner he had, like an intelligent setter. "Look, Mary Grace—"

"And stop calling me that."

"It's your name."

"No, it isn't." *Mary Grace*, whispered into her ear while he slid his hand up her body to cup her breast, that hand with the calluses at the tips of the fingers. She should have known then his mistress—music—had marked him. "I told you no one calls me that. Now, I'm certainly not meeting you later, so let's settle what kind of performance you'd like to give. I'll need to clear room on the schedule and set up a stage. There isn't a lot of time, because the event's this coming Sunday."

"No stage."

"I beg your pardon?"

"I figure the fundraiser's being held here at the museum for a reason. So"—he waved a hand—"let's keep the ambiance. I'll set up in the kitchen of one of the houses, make it a real old-time ceilidh. Which house is your favorite?"

Grace's heart skipped a beat. "The one nearest the water."

"I'll set up there, then."

No, not there. Grace had slept in that house too often, fantasized about it being her own snug home with her husband sleeping beside her and little ones tucked into their beds. And the husband? Always Brendan.

Don't ruin that dream for me.

But he kept right on talking. "I'll pull together a few other musicians. When Darcy comes back I'll ask if her boyfriend's in."

"He'll be thrilled."

"And I think I can rustle up a bodhran player and—what do you think—maybe accordion?"

"Maybe." She realized he was looking forward to the opportunity. "How long since you've played?"

He made a face. "Too long. The fingers get itchy, you know?"

She did. Her heart sank. He'd never change. Had she really imagined he might?

Chapter Seven

Mrs. Taylor popped out of her front door and caught Brendan just as he arrived home. The old lady had a head full of gray curls, eyes which tended to roll like those of a balky horse, and wire-rimmed glasses that continually slid down her nose. As a contemporary of his grandparents, she'd been known to Brendan all his life.

She spoke to him in a stage whisper. "Come in for a minute, Brendan, do."

He froze with his key stuck in his parents' lock. Now at late afternoon, he felt the effects of interrupted sleep and time spent in Mary Grace's company. He'd hoped to snatch a nap, but Mrs. Taylor insisted, "I need a word with you."

He gave a mental shrug and put a good face on it. "Something I can do for you, Mrs. Taylor?"

She ran her wild eyes up and down him in a shocking fashion. Surely that wasn't speculation he saw? But she said, "Rather something I can do for you, I expect."

The interior of her house looked and felt as different from his parents' as night from day. His ma favored deep, rich, jewel colors—like the garnet she'd painted Brendan's room—with contrasting white woodwork and traditional furnishings.

Mrs. Taylor's place looked like a box of flowers

had exploded in a cave. Fat roses covered the carpet, spiraled over the chesterfield, and even crawled up the walls. It didn't help that the old lady kept the drapes shut on the street side of the parlor and the place lay steeped in gloom.

"Come in and sit down. Will you take some tea?"

"Well, I don't think…"

"I made butter tarts."

That stopped Brendan in his tracks. His eyes picked out a tray on the coffee table, loaded with a tea service and a platter of pastries. How could he refuse?

"Well, now, I do love butter tarts."

"I know you do. I remember you as a child, when your mother would bring you over with your brother and sister. You just couldn't get enough of my butter tarts. And you've certainly grown up into a *handsome* young man. Sit down, Brendan. What are your brother and sister up to these days?"

Brendan parked himself on the chesterfield, resigned to a lengthy stay. "Well, you know Tom's out in B.C. Wife and four kids."

Mrs. Taylor beamed. "Your mother's shown me pictures. And Bella?"

"She's in Whitehorse—three kids."

"It's too bad for your parents all three of you strayed so far." Mrs. Taylor poured the tea as she spoke—piping hot. How had she known what time he'd come home? Had she kept the pot warmed while waiting to pounce on him like a spider? "And help yourself there, lad, to the butter tarts."

Brendan did. With the first bite, his eyes squinted shut in ecstasy. Better than sex—almost.

"Mrs. Taylor, you make the best tarts in the

44

world—flat out—and I've been around."

She simpered. "Oh, go on with you."

"No, I mean it." He helped himself to a second. "What's your secret? You put some magic in here, right?"

"Well, there is a secret ingredient. I've never told anyone what it is except my niece, Jenny, and my late husband, Dan. You remember Dan, don't you, Brendan?"

"I do, a bit."

"You were awfully young when he died. Taken in the prime of life he was—in the full flush of his manhood, you might say."

Brendan froze and stared at the old woman. "You don't mean—"

"Oh, I do. We enjoyed quite robust marital relations, and Dan put it all down to those tarts. Why, he'd consumed five of them just before...well, God rest him."

Brendan eyed the half-eaten tart in his hand. "What's in them? You can tell me."

"I'm afraid I can't."

"I promise it won't go any farther."

She gave a girlish laugh. "Trust me, it's something commonly found around the house, at least in a non-Methodist home."

Non-Methodist. Must be some kind of alcohol then. Brendan scrutinized the treat in his fingers more closely. He'd consumed various beverages from Texas to Yellow Knife. This probably wouldn't kill him.

Mrs. Taylor lowered her voice. "Dan always insisted those tarts acted like an aphrodisiac."

"And he ate five of them that night, you say?"

Then a mere three shouldn't hurt him, Brendan. He popped the rest of the tart into his mouth.

Still, an aphrodisiac? Surely his aged neighbor didn't have designs on him?

"So Brendan, what about you?"

"I beg your pardon, Mrs. Taylor?"

"Your brother has four children, your sister three. Doesn't that make you wish for a brood of your own?"

"Not really, Mrs. Taylor."

"Time's a-wasting, you know. You're fast approaching thirty."

"Not that fast."

"And now that you're back in St. John's, don't you think it's time to settle?"

"I'm not back for good, you understand. Just till the folks get home."

"Yes, but I heard a rumor your musical group broke up. And that's the only reason you didn't marry Grace Dawe, isn't it?"

Was it? Had he ever intended to marry Mary Grace? Only from the first time they'd kissed, and with his every heartbeat. If only she'd been reasonable about the music.

"I don't know about that."

"Never mind. There are hundreds of fish in the sea. Hundreds of mermaids." Mrs. Taylor waved a hand. "I'll soon have you fixed up with the perfect girl."

"Mrs. Taylor, I don't want—"

"I intend to introduce you to my niece."

"I can certainly find my own—"

"She's actually my great-niece. A fine, healthy girl, Jenny, with plenty for a man to get hold of, if you know what I mean. A hard worker, as well as dutiful. Why, she never stops coming by here to check on me, and I know she'd love to meet you."

Brendan paled. "Oh, Mrs. Taylor, I'm sure she's very—"

"And"—the old woman leaned toward him—"she has proper hips."

"What's that?"

"They run in the family." Mrs. Taylor arose from her comfy chair and wiggled her ample hips at him in a shocking fashion. "Made for bearing children, these hips. Why, Jenny could produce you half a dozen children, easy as you please."

Brendan choked on a stray crumb.

"Back in my day, a man looked for qualities like that in a woman."

"I—I'm sure. I'm surprised your Jenny hasn't been snatched right up, in that case."

"That's where you're in luck. She's only nineteen. I could arrange it so you get first chance at her, Brendan O'Rourke. Why, she already has a terrible, fierce crush on you."

"A crush?"

"That's what she calls it. In my day we *fancied* a fellow, but it amounts to the same thing."

Brendan's survival instinct kicked in. "Mrs. Taylor, while I'm sure your great-niece is a paragon, a veritable paragon of virtue, I'm not looking for a girl right now."

"Oh, what a pity. Jenny will be ever so disappointed."

"I'm sorry about that."

"She has no idea whatsoever that you prefer fellas. And frankly, what a waste." Mrs. Taylor eyed him very frankly indeed. "A good-looking man like yourself."

"Oh, no, you've got it all wrong. I can assure you I do prefer women. But—"

"That's all right then. Come by tomorrow for dinner. I'll have Jenny here. Say, five o'clock? And take the rest of the butter tarts with you." She wagged her eyebrows at him. "A bit of encouragement, so to say."

****

Back in his parents' house, Brendan set the remaining butter tarts in the center of the kitchen table and backed off warily, as if they might detonate. He hoped the effects of the three he'd eaten would pass quickly; the last thing he needed was another reason to be up all night.

Hearty laughter erupted throughout the room, and Charlie O'Rourke appeared, guffawing crudely.

"Caught in a right net now, aren't you, lad?"

"You heard? Can you believe that old woman? I thought she meant to seduce me right there on the chesterfield. Then she trots out the prospect of the niece. Not sure which is worse."

Charlie eased a chair out from the table without touching it and sat down. "That old woman's a caution. Killed that husband of hers, you know—with over-zealous relations."

"You're kidding."

"I am not. Wore the man out. They used to go at it like rabbits—could hear them through the walls."

"My God! She looks so sweet."

"Don't you believe it, lad. And she's had three lovers since old Dan."

"Three!"

"Killed them all. Last one was a fisherman—died

with his boots on. Heart attack. They was all heart attacks."

Brendan laid a hand on his chest. "It wasn't the butter tarts, was it?"

"No, lad—it was what came after."

"God! Have you seen the niece?"

"I have. Enough like Martha when she was young to raise the hairs on the back o' your neck. Stay clear of that, lad."

"She's invited me for supper tomorrow night."

"Then make some excuse. You want a woman, but not that one."

"I don't want a woman."

Charlie nodded at the plate of butter tarts. "You will when them kicks in."

"What's in 'em, do you know?" Brendan could hardly believe he sat in his parents' kitchen holding a casual conversation about seduction with a spirit, yet it suddenly seemed the most ordinary part of his day. Charlie O'Rourke was here; he'd better deal with it.

"I do not. But she keeps it in a wee bottle, and it smells an awful lot like Scotch."

"I see. When she called me in and said there was something she could do for me, I imagined she had a way to get rid of you."

Charlie's expression sobered. "Only one way to get rid of me, lad."

Brendan brightened. "What's that?"

"I need forgiveness for my sins. And you're going to gain that for me by earning forgiveness for yours."

Chapter Eight

Grace stood on the rocks at the edge of the outport, watching the ocean breathe. Night hung over the eastern horizon, but it hadn't yet reached her here on her perch. She reveled in the twilight, and its accompanying peace.

The waves made a hollow *thunk* on the boulders that lined the shore. The scents of salt and seaweed filled her nostrils, and a breeze played with the long skirt of her dress. Behind her the museum lay empty, everyone gone—but her and Cabot—and the day put to rest.

What a day it had been.

Now she just needed to get Brendan O'Rourke out of her head and replace him with some of this peace.

She wondered if she could. Darcy had never stopped talking about him after he left the office. How warm he'd been, how down-to-earth, how handsome. How kind it was of him to play at the fundraiser. How much more attractive he was in person than in his publicity pictures.

He was. Oh, he was. Not that Grace had any publicity pictures—she'd refused to collect them. But she couldn't go into a shop around town without seeing the band's CDs prominently displayed, along with an occasional poster. St. John's was justifiably proud of its home-grown stars.

He'd made it big, damn him. He'd gone off and left her, made the choice she'd thrown at him that night, and climbed to success.

She had to admit she hadn't believed he would. Not that she doubted his talent—no one who heard him play could. She just hadn't believed he could walk away from her and stay away.

She thought the love would call him back, even above the lure of the music and yes, fame.

The fact that it hadn't still hurt so much that the ocean blurred before her eyes.

Oh, God, why hadn't she cured herself by now? Why couldn't she rid herself of wanting him? If she were brutally honest, she had to admit even now she ached for him to come walking back into her life desperate for her, and say—

"Grace?"

The voice came from behind her, close behind. She caught her breath and spun around on the rocks so quickly she teetered and nearly fell into the ocean.

The man reached out and caught her by the elbow. Dusk had gathered after all, and she couldn't see him clearly. But as soon as he touched her she identified him.

"Chet. What are you doing here?"

"We need to talk. Grace, I can't help but think we can still work through whatever made you call off the wedding. If you'll just give me another chance—"

Grace. Brendan would have called her Mary Grace. She fought down her disappointment and drew a breath. "Chet, we've been over all this."

"No, we haven't, not really, because we've not got to the bottom of it."

51

"It isn't about me giving you another chance. You've done nothing wrong. I keep telling you that."

"I know, but—damn it, I'm still in love with you."

All Grace's defiance crumbled; she collapsed inside. The tears she'd been holding back for Brendan trickled from her eyes. "I don't know why. I honestly don't. I've treated you so badly."

"It doesn't matter. I want you back again."

Somebody wanted her. That seductive call had drawn her to Chet in the first place. A good man—if a bit stodgy—he'd offered her what Brendan hadn't.

A hell of a reason to get married. That truth had at last come home to her—almost too late.

She shook her head wildly. "I don't deserve you, I don't—"

He pulled her into his arms. And it felt good having someone hold her there in the gathering dark with the sound of the water all around. It didn't answer the need inside her—that for another man—but it blunted the hurt.

"Don't cry, Grace. It'll be all right."

"How can you say that? How can you even come near me after what I did?"

Chet gazed into her face seriously. And he couldn't look less like Brendan O'Rourke if he tried, with his dark hair, brown eyes, and plain, broad face that contained no devilment whatsoever.

"It was embarrassing, sure. Humiliating. I still have relatives calling me up asking what happened to the wedding and wondering about their presents."

"I've returned all the presents." Grace drew away from him and palmed her wet cheeks. "I did. And I paid the balance on the hall. What do you tell them all?"

"That it's a woman's prerogative to change her mind. That I'll be waiting when you change it back again."

Here was the steadiness, the constancy she'd craved and never found in Brendan O'Rourke. Why couldn't she accept the gift?

"But I won't."

"You will. You're just confused. Marriage is a big step."

"I refuse to let you cool your heels waiting for what's never going to happen, Chet. You deserve better, much better."

He didn't answer that directly. "Are you staying here tonight?"

"I don't know. I guess so."

"Let me stay with you. We need some time alone, no outside pressure. No wedding pressure. I'm sure that's what made you panic."

Panic. Yes, she had. She'd tried on her wedding gown for the last time before the ceremony, looked at herself in the mirror, and had a glimpse of a future that had made it impossible to breathe.

"Chet, it wasn't outside pressure. It was *me*."

She could see by the flicker of emotion in his eyes he didn't like that. "You mean me."

"No, I—"

"Because that's what women always say when they decide there's something wrong with a fella. What is it, Grace? I'm too dull? Too predictable?" An edge came to his voice. "I'm not Brendan O'Rourke?"

Grace swayed as if she'd been struck. Up to this moment Chet had betrayed little anger or hurt. Now it came rushing.

"I hear he's back in town. Have you seen him?"

"That's not…" Grace caught herself. In truth Brendan was the reason she'd backed out of the wedding. And how pitiful was that? She'd given up a stellar man for one who didn't want her.

Fool, fool, fool.

Of all the things Chet deserved, he deserved her honesty.

"I've seen him. Father Hurley's wrangled him into playing here on Sunday, as a matter of fact. And I have to admit there are still some feelings there."

"On his side, or yours?"

Grace swallowed her own bitter pill of humiliation. "Mine. He doesn't care. He walked out on me years ago, Chet. But it's hard."

"Yeah, it is." Chet gave a pained smile. "Hard seeing the person you still love, hoping there'll be a spark of…something left." Chet turned away, and quickly swung back again. "It was good between us for a while, Grace. Tell me I didn't imagine that."

"It was, Chet. It was good."

"It could be again."

She let his words hang out there, unwilling to crush them. They represented her own sentiments, but not toward this man.

She said with passion, "I wish I could wave a magic wand and change things."

"Yeah, but Grace, if I gave you that wand, if I placed it in your hand right now, what would you change? Would you make it so you loved me? Or so he loved you?"

She said nothing, and the hurtful smile once more crossed his face. "And there's my answer. Is Cabot here with you?"

Grace nodded to where the big Newfoundland roamed up the shore. "Yes."

"Good. Because I still need to know you're safe."

She watched him walk away and stood on by the water till the darkness became complete.

Chapter Nine

"So what's all this about redemption?" Brendan asked the spirit of Charlie O'Rourke. "Spit it out, old man."

Charlie drew himself up in the chair. "Mind how you speak to me, lad. Respect is still due."

"Respect? You cause a fuss with the neighbors, keep me awake with that screeching fiddle of yours…"

"Screeching?"

"And turn up drunk. You're drunk now, aren't you?"

"Well, lad, let me tell you a little secret about the afterlife. Right from the horse's mouth, so to speak. It's not all what Father Hurley would have you believe."

"No?"

"Decidedly not. We build the men we are, see, while we live our lives—day by day, hour by hour, minute by minute. It's a bit like wax running down a candle. You know how it goes all lumpy and drippy?"

"I do."

"Well, when the flame snuffs out"—Charlie waved a ghostly hand—"the candle sort of freezes in that form. No more changing—you're stuck with what you have."

Brendan frowned. As an analogy, it lacked something.

"So when I winked out at the fine young age of thirty-two, I froze more or less where I was—on a spiritual level, you understand. A reprobate. A waster. Drunk. So now I'm still all those things—but aching to redeem myself."

Brendan didn't like this.

"And lad, I'm stuck with all the remorse I should have felt then. Only now I've an eternity to contemplate it."

"That sucks." Brendan opened a bottle of beer—he'd found his father's stash on the back porch after all—and took a swig. "Have you been here in this house since you died?"

"I have. In the attic, mostly. Keeping out of the way."

"It's a damn small attic," Brendan reflected.

"It is. Also cold and lonely. But having caused enough grief in life, I did not want to bother my descendants."

"That was considerate of you."

"I've a lot to make up for, lad."

"So are you stuck here forever?"

"I hope not. 'Tis a terrible drear thing, being tied to a place. There's old Robbie Caine over on Forest Road—he's grounded like me, only the house got tore down. Now he's haunting a row of trash bins."

"I don't think that will happen to you." Brendan took another swig and glanced around the room. "Ma and Pa love this place too much."

"That's little comfort." Charlie snorted. "Especially when I contemplate the fact that you're likely to inherit the house."

"Me? Oh, no. There's three of us."

"Your brother and sister will never come home, at least not to stay. And your parents can't let the house pass out of the family, not after all my Bridget went through to hold onto it after I abandoned her."

"What did she go through?"

"Only think of it, lad—left a widow at a mere twenty-three years and with a babe in arms. Ah, and she was a beauty in them days—red hair that flowed near down to her knees, cheeks like roses, breasts—"

"Er, that *is* my great-grandmother you're describing."

"A veritable goddess. And to what did I reduce her? Charring for other folks. Counting pennies like they were rubies. Taking in strangers."

"Taking in strangers?"

"She had no choice but to turn this place into a boardinghouse for a while. Worked day and night—made herself old before her time. My fault. It was all my fault."

Charlie fell into brooding silence. Brendan contemplated it and took another swig. "Yes, I guess you have a lot to answer for. And it seems Bridget's the one deserving my respect. I take it she's not here as well."

"No," Charlie moaned. "She's gone on where the deserving go."

"Where's that?"

"Well, I'll tell you, lad, because it's something you can aim for while you set about redeeming your own soul."

"I'm not redeeming my soul. It's in fine fettle."

"It isn't. That's why I appeared to you in the first place. If I can do some good in my suffering, I'm all for it."

"A martyr, are you?"

"Nothing of the kind. I'm hoping if I can reform myself and accomplish some good, I'll win my way free to go find Bridget and beg her forgiveness."

"Not sure I'd forgive you, if I were her."

"Me either," Charlie admitted gloomily.

"But you were telling me about where she's gone."

"Well, lad, you know the sea."

"I should."

"There's another sea like it in the spiritual realm—a great sea o' light. There lies all happiness, fulfillment, joy, and peace. I've caught glimpses of it, but that's all."

"That's where she's gone?"

"It is, and deservedly."

"And you think if you could get free of your guilt you could find her there?"

"I'd never stop looking."

"And you suppose she'll want you to join her after all you did?"

"That's the question. It's the kind of place where anger and thoughts of revenge sort of flit away. So I'm hoping."

"No drink there, I'll bet. You ready for that?"

"More than ready."

"But you haven't been sober in—what, nearly eighty years?"

"Watch your lip, or I'll give you a smack with that bottle. Don't think I can't. Isn't it bad enough you sit there drinking and torturing me for want of a taste?"

"Sorry." Brendan set the bottle down. "Tell what you have to do in order to get free, and what it has to do with me."

"All these years, I haven't been sure what to do in

59

order to redeem myself or how to win back my Bridget's love. Then you turned up and gave me the answer."

"I'm the answer?"

"Hard to believe, ain't it? A wastrel like yourself. But you're so much like me, and I don't mean just to look at. You've made the same mistakes. But whereas you're not dead—"

"Yet."

"Yet, you still have a chance to set things right. And I'm hoping if I can make you see the errors of your ways, Bridget will see my heart has truly changed."

"The band, you mean."

"No, I'm not talking about your bloody band but about Mary Grace Dawe."

"Oh, now—" Brendan held up a hand. "Not that."

"Precisely that. It's too late for me to do right by the woman I love, lad, but not for you."

"You're assuming I still love Mary Grace."

Charlie laughed. "I know you do. See, I understand you as no one else ever will—I know what drives you and what lies underneath it all. The music drives you, just as it did me. But the woman lies in your heart."

"With all due respect, butt out. I'm over her. Have been for years."

"Did you know your aura changes when you lie?"

"My what, then?"

"It's a sort of curtain of light that hangs around you. Yours is normally a pretty orange color—until you lie, when it turns blackish."

"I'll always have feelings for her, sure. She was my first love."

"To borrow your word, 'bullshit.' You're as much

in love with the girl now as the first time you kissed her. Just like I'm as much in love as ever with my beautiful Bridget. It's how we O'Rourke men are. Your father and grandfather were smart enough to realize when they had a good thing. You and I? Stupid—abysmally stupid." Charlie leaned toward Brendan across the table. "I spend all my time drunk. What is your excuse?"

Brendan tapped his fingers on the table. "It's over between me and Mary Grace. I'm not raking all that up again. And I'm sure as hell not going crawling back to her, apologizing for—"

"For what? Breaking her heart? Trust me, lad, it's better to crawl now than regret it for eternity."

"It was her choice to break up. She couldn't accept that music takes first place in my life."

"She might have accepted that, if you'd presented it in the right way. My Bridget did. What poor Mary Grace couldn't accept was you making a choice of it."

"No, you've got it wrong. She gave me an ultimatum."

"All you would have had to say was you couldn't live without her and she'd have let you play. It's what women want, lad—it's all they want, to be first in the heart of the man they love. It's all Bridget wanted, and I saw that too late."

"Mary Grace wanted to change me. I'll never change."

"Just as I haven't—to my sorrow. Just as, now, I maybe never can."

Brendan directed an evil stare at the ghost opposite him. "Well, I can tell you one thing's going to change. I've arranged for Father Hurley to come in and do an exorcism."

"That sanctimonious old toad?" Charlie guffawed.

"Holy water and all."

"Let him sprinkle away! Don't you know I was excommunicated years ago? His puffery will have no effect on me."

Chapter Ten

"Well that's a lame excuse and no mistake."
Charlie spoke the words in Brendan's ear and sent a
shiver down his spine.

The next day had come, and Brendan had just
finished telling Mrs. Taylor he'd forgotten a promise to
play fiddle down at Fitzgerald's; they'd need to
postpone supper to another night.

The last thing he needed was one more marathon
conversation with Charlie.

He snapped, "It's not an excuse. You see this fiddle
in my hand? I'm off now to play, aren't I?"

"And just as well. Too long since you've touched
that instrument, caressed her as she deserves. Makes a
fellow jittery; I know."

"My fiddle is not an addiction. It's my livelihood."

"Tell yourself that, son."

"I'm going to Fitzgerald's Pub, and you needn't
come with me."

"I can't come with you," Charlie answered
gloomily. "Anchored here."

Thank God.

The old man would be the death of him. Following
their all-too-personal discussion last night—and three
pilfered beers—Brendan had taken to his bed and
snatched about an hour's sleep, only to be wakened
around four by a fiery rendition of the "March of the

King of Laois."

He wanted to find out if he could play the tune that well and meant to try it out at Fitzgerald's.

Charlie leaned forward. "A word in your ear before you go."

"Can I stop you?"

"The solution to your problem with Mrs. Taylor? Barry Tate."

"I beg your pardon?"

"How did you get so thick, lad? The man never stops hankering after women."

"You want me to fix Barry up with Mrs. Taylor?"

"No, you cloth-eared twit. With the niece."

"Jenny?"

"Ask if you can bring Barry with you to supper. Martha will never say no—two men being better than one. Barry and the niece are perfect for one another."

"Are they?"

"I'm surprised you can't see it."

A matchmaking ghost. Well, well. "A good idea. Thanks."

He arrived at Fitzgerald's early, having sloped off with his fiddle directly after making his excuses to Mrs. Taylor and shrugging off Charlie, but found a number of old acquaintances present. He let them buy him several beers before cracking open his fiddle case, all while keeping his eye on a blonde in the corner.

A luscious thing, she sat all alone nursing a drink, waiting for someone, most likely, and watching him, Brendan.

Brendan asked the bartender, "Who's that over there?"

"Don't know. Came in by herself a short while ago.

You interested?"

Brendan shook his head ruefully. "Last thing I need right now is another complication."

"Looks like she's interested."

"Ah, she's just passing her time. Not much else to look at in this place."

"Thanks." The bartender, a fellow named Devon, grinned. "I was getting all the action in here till you came in."

"Maybe she's looking at you, after all."

Devon shrugged. "Pretty enough. I'd take her home with me."

An hour later, Brendan knew it wasn't the bartender capturing the lovely blonde's attention. Devon had ended his shift and gone home, to be replaced behind the bar by Margie. Brendan broke out his fiddle and played several tunes, drawing a small crowd that included Barry Tate. Everyone bought him drinks, and he began to slip into that happy place wherein thought went away and instinct—including that which allowed him to play—reigned supreme.

This was where his fingers limbered, his brain hummed, and the strings caught fire. It took him a moment to realize the blonde had abandoned her table and stood next to his.

"Amazing," she said during a lull. "You're just amazing."

Brendan grinned at her. He'd just finished playing the "March of the King of Laois" even better than his great-grandfather, or so he believed. "You think so?"

"I know so. I'd buy you a drink, but I see that's been done. Maybe I can offer something else."

Brendan looked into her eyes, ice blue and frankly

speculative.

Well, now.

"Let's not get ahead of ourselves, my love. The night's young. Why don't you sit down and tell me your name?"

"Stephanie Contrelle."

"You're not from 'round here, are you?"

"No, I'm from Montreal. I traveled here to St. John's with a friend who's visiting home. Betsy Grant—do you know her?"

Brendan shrugged. "I've been away a while myself. So you came here tonight on your own?"

"Betsy's at a family reunion. I came looking for adventure." She held his gaze for several heartbeats. "I think I found it."

Well, well.

"Have a drink." He waved a hand at the wide array on the table.

"I think I will. Your ale is very different from what we drink at home."

"Ale's ale, darling." And it helped the process along. Did he want to take her home with him? He liked the excitement of the idea, and it might help him sleep later. Wished he could say he'd never had a woman who spoke French in his ear, but he had—in Montreal.

"So what do you do back home?"

"I'm a coiffeur—a hair stylist. But I don't want to talk about me. Tell you the truth, I don't want to talk at all. They"—she gestured at the crowd at the bar—"say you're a famous musician."

"Lately of a group called Kissin' the Cod."

"I have heard of you. On the radio." The speculation in her eyes deepened. Suddenly Brendan felt like a lion caught in the sights of a big game hunter. Did she need a musician to mount on her wall?

Who cared if she did? She might be just what he needed, in turn.

He leaned forward to land a kiss on her cheek. "Hang around till I finish, eh?"

She turned her head so her lips met his. "I will."

Three hours later, they left the bar and reeled up George Street toward Garland, with the stars bright overhead. Brendan wondered whether Stephanie was as drunk as he. He didn't think so; she had her arm threaded through his and tottered on her heels, but she seemed to know what she was doing.

Brendan tried to convince himself he did too, and failed. He'd spent the past hours with one eye on Stephanie's cleavage and the other on the door. Now he tried to pretend he hadn't been hoping Mary Grace would come in.

Mary Grace. Why couldn't he get her out of his head? Now he realized she'd always been there, even when he traveled the country.

At the corner of George and Garland Streets, Stephanie backed him against the side of a building and kissed him. Her tongue darted into his mouth with dominance that almost frightened him.

What ho! He very nearly dropped his fiddle. It was going to be one of *those* nights.

He gasped at her, "Wait now, till we get home."

"Don't you want me?"

"Sure I do."

"Then it shouldn't matter where. Haven't you ever done it on a street corner?"

"Does inside a cab count?"

"*Non.*"

"Then, no. Look, the house is just up this street. Sure you can wait a minute."

At his door, he fumbled with the key and feared she'd jump him again. Inside, he set his fiddle in the hall.

"Where's the bed, Brendan?"

"Upstairs."

"Come on."

She bolted up quickly for a girl in four-inch heels. When she made for his parents' room at the top of the stairs, he tugged her into his instead.

By then she was panting and pawing at him. "Hurry."

"Easy, darling, we've got all night."

"But I am impatient."

"No kidding."

She shed her clothes in record time and stood outlined in the muddy light from the window. And what a body—full in all the right places, with long legs and heavy breasts.

He gulped on a sudden rush of pure lust. Maybe this was a good idea after all.

So long as she didn't hurt him.

"Take off your clothes and get on the bed."

Brendan shed his shirt, shucked his pants.

"Hmm." She licked her lips. "Nice. Just so you know, I like it doggie-style."

Jaysus. He stayed where he was and bleated, "Do you? Really? I've always thought face-to-face is nicer. We can gaze into one another's eyes."

"You're drunk."

"Am I?"

"*Oui*, but I don't mind. Me, I am not so interested in your eyes as..." She flicked him with a speaking glance.

"Oh, right, my love. I've got that covered, as well."

"I can see that you have."

She sprang onto Brendan's bed, and he remained rooted to the floor, wondering why he hesitated. He could manage doggie-style. He'd done that before, though with this damn fog in his head he couldn't quite remember when.

He laughed.

"What's so funny?" she asked over her shoulder.

"We should do it horsey-style. That would make me a stallion."

"*Oui*, and so you are. Now come here and perform."

"Sure." Funny how he could still get it up even when he was this drunk. He supposed that's what stallions did.

And maybe if he followed through with this he could get Mary Grace out of his head for good.

"Monsieur Brendan, are you coming or not?" Stephanie addressed him again and then froze on the bed, mouth gaping. Her eyes and lips became perfectly round. "*Mon Dieu!* What is that?"

"What? Where?"

She pointed behind Brendan, and he whirled. There up against the wall, light swirled in a small vortex. A reflection from outside? From the mirror? No. For even as he stared the light coalesced into the vague outline of a body topped by a hideous head complete with contorted face.

"Aarrgghh!" the face uttered, and Stephanie

squealed. She contracted into a ball on the bed.

"What is that?"

"Oh, that? It's nothing."

"It is not nothing! Is this some trick? Did you bring me here to murder me?"

"No, to be sure not. It's just my great-grandfather. He's dead and can't really bother us, I promise. Might want to watch, it being doggie-style and all. Not sure he saw much of that in his day. But on second thought, he must have. The Greeks…"

"Shut up!"

"I'm just saying—"

"Shut up, shut up! You are telling me there's a ghost? You have a ghost in this house?"

Charlie chose that moment to lunge forward. "Give us a kiss, dearie." He leered. "I'll show you doggie-style."

"Switch on the light! Give me my clothes! I am not staying here."

Brendan gathered up her panties and bra. "If you insist."

"I do!" Hastily she dressed, never taking her gaze from Charlie, who hovered two feet off the floor, and keeping Brendan between her and the ghost. "This is a madhouse. This never happened, do you understand? I was never here."

"I've got it. Just let me—"

"You stay where you are. I will see myself out. I hope never to see you again."

She flew out; the bedroom door slammed, followed by the one downstairs, rattling the windows.

Brendan, ale fumes quickly clearing from his head, turned on Charlie.

"You'd better have a damned good explanation."

"The best, lad. I just saved you from yourself."

"Is that so?"

"Yes, and you can thank me in the morning. Because you don't want that, son. You want Mary Grace Dawe."

Chapter Eleven

Grace, with Cabot at her side, had just finished conducting a tour for yet another school group when she saw the tall man approaching through the sunshine. Something about the smooth lope at which he moved snared her attention, as did the gleam of red in his hair. Attraction whipped through her even before she recognized Brendan O'Rourke.

The last person she wanted to see.

The school children trailed away to their bus, and she stood watching Brendan draw nearer, helplessly admiring the long legs and narrow hips encased in black denim, and the pleasing lines of his face.

Annoyance at her own failure to squash her feelings made her call out, "What are you doing here? I didn't expect to see you till Sunday."

"There's been a snag." He reached her and shuffled to a halt, his shoulders hunched and his hands thrust into his pockets. "I'm not sure I'll be able to perform."

"Oh, now, look here. I've already reorganized the schedule once at late notice and reprinted the fliers. You're not bagging off on me." Again.

"It's not that. I want to play, Mary Grace. It's just someone's stolen my fiddle."

"Isolde?" He'd had that fiddle forever—since he'd started playing professionally. "How'd that happen? I suppose you had her down the bar."

"I did, yes."

"You must have noticed someone walking off with her."

"It wasn't quite like that."

"What was it like?"

"A house guest walked off with her."

"A house guest." Grace's brain translated that from man-speak. "You had a woman in? And she stole your fiddle?"

"I'd left it in the hall, see, when we came in."

Grace flushed—with anger, so she told herself. "Anxious to get upstairs, I'll warrant."

"I was under orders. She wasn't a nice woman."

"And you were drunk. Seems to me you got what you deserved."

"That's hard, Mary Grace."

"And it doesn't matter. There are other fiddles. You'll find one by Sunday. Two whole days."

"No, I won't."

"You mean to tell me there are no other fiddles in St. John's?"

"Not like Isolde. Mary Grace, you know she's special."

"I do know that. But you could actually *play another instrument*. Brendan O'Rourke"—she stamped her foot—"you are *not* letting me down."

"No, Mary Grace."

She gritted her teeth. "And don't call me that." Seeing the misery in his eyes, she relented. "Do you know this woman's name?"

"Yes."

"And have you reported the theft to the police?"

"I have, yes."

Grace blew out a breath. "Then maybe they'll find Isolde before Sunday. What does Father Hurley say?"

Brendan made a face. "I haven't had the nerve to tell Father Hurley, what with the circumstances and all."

"So you came and told me instead. You thought I'd be more sympathetic?"

"I did not."

She waved a finger in his face. "I hope they find her, I really do. But you will admit this was caused by your own rash stupidity."

"It was, yes."

"I hope she was worth it, this wanton thief."

"She wasn't. We didn't even—"

Grace snorted and flicked him up and down with a glance. "You expect me to believe that?" What woman—even a thief—could get her hands on him and then walk away without taking full advantage?

"It's the truth."

"Well, I don't believe you."

He shrugged. "You never did, Mary Grace Dawe. You never heard half the things I told you."

She froze with Cabot's big head beneath her hand. "What's that?"

He shook his head. "Never mind."

"No, I want you to explain."

"If we talk about the past, we'll quarrel, and I didn't come here for that."

She stared into his eyes. "Give me one thing you ever told me that I didn't believe."

"That I loved you. If you'd believed that—really believed what it meant when I said it—nothing could have come between us."

74

"The music—"

"Not even the music."

Grace's heart thudded to her feet. She remembered that last argument so well, the one that had split them. Every word had repeated in her mind a thousand times. He had said he loved her. But he hadn't showed it by promising to be there when she needed him, by being willing to put her first at least part of the time.

Had she been wrong? Had she failed to listen? Defensiveness made her strike out. "Brendan O'Rourke, don't you try and turn it 'round on me, saying our split was my fault."

He shook his head. "This is hopeless. Talking reasonably to you was always hopeless."

"Then why did you come?"

"To tell you about Isolde. And to invite you to supper, followed by an exorcism."

"You're inviting me to supper? Are you mad?"

"Don't get too excited. It's at Mrs. Taylor's house. She's—"

"I remember who she is."

"Right. She wants to introduce me to her great-niece."

"And you want a shield."

"Two shields, actually. Barry will be there, too. He's a decoy for Jenny, the grand-niece. That was Charlie's idea."

"Charlie?"

"My great-grandfather. The ghost."

"That's right, you said he speaks to you."

"Oh, Mary Grace, you should hear the conversations we've had." Brendan waved his hand. "Far-reaching and philosophical."

"You're still drunk."

"Not a bit of it." He added confidingly, "He'll be gone anyway, after tonight. I thought you just might enjoy the exorcism."

"I don't know what to say."

"Say you'll come. We can at least be friends. If my visit home accomplishes only one thing, let it be that we are still friends."

Could she be this man's friend and nothing more? No, no, no, no. Impossible. Even now, standing here with him in the sunshine, annoyed and wary, she wanted him.

"I'll think about it."

"You'll come—for old time's sake. Five o'clock." He winked at her. "And a word of warning: don't eat the butter tarts."

****

Grace found a parking space on Duckworth Street and walked back to the O'Rourkes' just in time to see Barry Tate disappearing into the house next door. She'd nearly reached it when Brendan emerged and saw her. He paused while a big smile spread across his face.

"Thank God."

She huffed to a stop beside him. "I don't know why I'm here." Maybe because he looked so good—damn it, he did—clad in a deep green dress shirt, with his hair for once disciplined. It wouldn't stay that way, she knew. Brendan O'Rourke's hair had a life of its own.

The smile in his eyes deepened. "Maybe you just can't resist the chance to witness an actual exorcism?"

"I don't think that's it. Are you sure Mrs.—"

The door of Mrs. Taylor's house swung open behind Brendan, and the old lady poked her head out.

"Are you coming, Brendan O'Rourke?"

"Good news, Mrs. Taylor. The other guest was able to come after all. I'm sure you remember Mary Grace Dawe."

"I certainly do. Well, Mary Grace—"

"It's Grace; just Grace."

Mrs. Taylor didn't look markedly pleased to see her. And Brendan O'Rourke once more proved himself a rapscallion. He bargained on the Newfoundlander's native hospitality, which kicked in despite Mrs. Taylor's obvious displeasure.

"Of course you're welcome, my dear."

The old lady ushered them in where the scents of a traditional boiled dinner met Grace's nostrils.

"You see," Brendan told Mrs. Taylor as they went, "I bumped into Mary Grace this afternoon and couldn't help but mention how much I was looking forward to supper tonight. I'm afraid I talked up your cooking quite a bit."

"It smells wonderful," Grace put in truthfully.

Mrs. Taylor rolled an eye at Brendan. "I told you Jenny's preparing supper tonight. My niece," she added for Grace's benefit as she led them into the dining room.

"Jenny, set another place at the table, will you, girl?"

Jenny, who'd been making awkward conversation with Barry Tate, jerked to life and hurried off into the kitchen.

Barry Tate grinned and nodded at Grace. "Hello, Grace. Never expected to see you here."

"Brendan's been talking up the butter tarts."

Mrs. Taylor gave her a sharp look. "No butter tarts

tonight, I'm afraid. Jenny's made one of her magnificent trifles for dessert."

"My favorite," Barry enthused as Jenny came back into the room. The girl gave him a smile.

She was pretty, Grace decided, in an innocent, round-faced way, with long, mouse-brown hair and a figure that one day would probably resemble that of her well-padded great-aunt.

Brendan edged up to Grace. "Don't mention the exorcism later. And sit next to me."

Why, the big baby, Grace thought.

It did him no good anyway, for when Mrs. Taylor handed out the table assignments, Jenny ended up flanked by Brendan and Barry, with Grace on her own across from them and Mrs. Taylor at the end.

"Isn't this cozy?" the old woman demanded. "Jenny, pass the dishes. Barry Tate, it's a pleasure to have you here—it's an age since I've seen you, young man. What have you been up to?"

Barry, bless him, launched into a longwinded, rambling account of his activities, how busy he was at work, and the various tours he'd run, complete with horror stories about some of the clients. Jenny hung on his every word, while Brendan remained silent except for a chuckle or two.

Not till Grace glanced up from her meal did she realize Brendan watched her intently from across the table, every movement, each bite she took.

What was he thinking? Had he forgotten Mrs. Taylor had arranged all this so he'd focus on Jenny?

As did Barry; with a start Grace realized that truth. Barry might have begun his conversation talking to all of them. Now he spoke directly to Jenny.

"You're so lucky to have an exciting job like that," Jenny enthused when he paused. "My job's so dull."

"What do you do, my love?"

"Waitress at the Happy Crab. So I deal with tourists too, in a way. But I've never had one fall overboard from a whale-watching boat. And I've never had a small boy kick me in the shins repeatedly because I asked him to sit down."

Barry widened his eyes. "Black and blue I was. For days."

"I'll just bet you were. How brave of you to stick to your guns."

Barry puffed his chest out a bit.

Brendan winked at Grace, a slow, seductive wink that almost made her choke on her potato. What was he thinking? Didn't he know Mrs. Taylor would notice? Grace bet the old lady noticed everything.

She cleared her throat. "So, Brendan, I hope you're looking forward to playing Sunday."

"I always look forward to playing, Mary Grace. You know that."

So she did, all too well. "Jenny, I hope you're planning on attending the fundraiser Sunday at the museum. You can keep our Brendan, here, company."

Brendan glared, and Jenny tore her gaze from Barry long enough to say, "Oh, of course I always try to support community events. Will you be there, Barry?"

"Question is, will Brendan's fiddle turn up by then." Barry, who unquestionably loved to talk, launched into an account of the theft, carefully expunged of sexual innuendo for Mrs. Taylor's benefit.

"She just walked off with it?" Jenny cried when he finished. "Why would she do such a thing?"

"Not a very nice person, obviously," Grace put in. "Brendan needs to be more careful about the people with whom he associates."

"Oh, yes, my dear," Mrs. Taylor enthused. "Especially the women—a young fella can't be too careful about women."

Now she embarked on a remembrance of all the black-widow types she'd met over the years.

"I hope they find your fiddle," Jenny fretted when her aunt finished, focusing at last on Brendan. "Whatever will you do about the fundraiser?"

"Find another fiddle, I suppose." Brendan looked at Grace. "I dare not let anyone down."

"Why don't you use Charlie's?" Mrs. Taylor asked.

"I beg your pardon?" That caught all Brendan's attention.

"It's supposed to be there somewhere in the house, or so I remember your grandmother saying."

"Is it so? Where?"

"Now, how would I know such a thing? I just recall hearing it said when Charlie O'Rourke died"—she leaned forward and lowered her voice—"and they picked him up from the street that night, it was the one thing of value he possessed."

Jenny stared. "They picked him up from the street, Auntie?"

"Oh, yes, girl. The man had been on a tear." Mrs. Taylor spoke as if it had happened yesterday. "Drinking himself to death, you see. Down and out doesn't begin to describe it. Charlie O'Rourke was bent on self-destruction."

"Well, now…" Brendan began.

"You hush, Brendan O'Rourke. You know nothing.

The rascal had already abandoned his wife and infant son"—she glared at Brendan accusingly, as if it were his fault—"to play down every dive in St. John's. And that poor wife of his, Bridget, a saint."

"Why didn't she divorce him?" Jenny asked.

"Divorce? Land sakes, girl, there was no such thing back then. Irish Catholics they were—not good Anglicans like us."

"Oh." Jenny's eyes rounded.

Mrs. Taylor went on, "They say Charlie O'Rourke ran amok that night. Of course he had a skinful, like always. But one minute he was kicking up his heels playing music. They say he played a last song—"The Parting Glass," it was—and up and ran out into the street with his fiddle. He suffered some sort of attack and fell down where he stood. They had to pry that fiddle out of his cold, dead hands."

Grace shot Brendan a speaking look.

"They wouldn't have been cold, surely," Barry put in. "Not that quick. It takes the body a certain amount of time to cool down."

"Never mind that," Mrs. Taylor snapped. "The point is that fiddle was the one thing he valued when he died. They carried it home to Bridget O'Rourke. She turned pale as milk and cradled the fiddle in her arms."

"You can't possibly know all this," Grace objected.

"It's legend. And even though it had been weeks since they lived together, and though poor Bridget needed every penny to support her baby, she refused to sell that fiddle. Not even to pay for a wake, which is why Charlie never had one."

"No wake?" Barry raised his eyebrows. "No wonder the poor beggar's still hanging about."

"So," Mrs. Taylor concluded, "you know the fiddle is still somewhere in the house. If Bridget wouldn't part with it, you can be sure no one else would."

"But where?" Jenny wondered. "Oh, Brendan, it's like a treasure hunt. I say we all go next door and look."

"After trifle," Mrs. Taylor stipulated.

"Well, but..." Brendan desperately tried to fend them off. "I never saw a hint of any fiddle, and I grew up there. No one mentioned it. And it would scarcely be playable anyway, after all this time. Especially if it's been put in the attic. The heat and cold would be fatal."

"Nonsense," said Barry. "What about those stories of people finding a Stradivarius?"

"Bring out the trifle, Jenny," Mrs. Taylor ordered. "We'll have dessert, and you can all go next door."

Chapter Twelve

"What was in that trifle?" Mary Grace leaned close and whispered the question into Brendan's ear. Her breath skittered down his neck, fanning passions that really didn't need any encouragement.

The two of them—alone at last—ostensibly searched the rear of a second-floor cupboard for Charlie O'Rourke's fiddle. In truth, most of Brendan's attention centered on Mary Grace.

"Brandy," he replied. "Lots of brandy. And, I suspect, Mrs. Taylor's secret ingredient—the same one she puts in the butter tarts."

"But she said Jenny made the trifle."

"I'm sure Mrs. Taylor shared her know-how. They're two of a kind. Can't you see it? In sixty years Jenny will look just like her great-aunt."

Brendan cocked an ear when a giggle floated down from the attic where Jenny and Barry supposedly searched together. Not much getting done up there either, it seemed.

Mary Grace leaned still closer. "They're like witches, two of the three witches in...what's-the-thingy?"

"MacBeth."

"Right, MacBeth. Why can't I think clearly?"

Neither could Brendan, especially with Mary Grace so close. "Must be the effects of the secret ingredient."

"But that doesn't account for the way you smell." Mary Grace stuck her face in his neck. "Why do you always smell so damn good?"

Brendan went very still. What would she do if he kissed her? Clout him on the side of the head, most likely.

"Hey, I have an idea," she burst out.

"That we should go to my room together?"

She gazed into his eyes. What did he see in hers? Lust? Brandy fumes? Rejection?

"No, not that."

"Do you remember the first time we were in my room together?"

"Your parents were away. Just like now." Mary Grace licked her lips. "You fancied you snuck me in, but I'll bet all your neighbors saw."

"I was so horny. And so scared. It was the first time—"

"For either of us. I was seventeen."

"Neither of us knew what we were doing."

"No," Mary Grace sighed, "but it came naturally, didn't it? It always came naturally with you."

"Like breathing." He leaned in till his lips hovered over hers. She eased forward into his arms.

From the attic came another giggle; Jenny pounded down the ladder with Barry in close pursuit. The girl's cheeks looked flushed, her eyes bright. Barry huffed like a steam train.

"Nothing up there," Jenny cried.

Mary Grace sprang away from Brendan and put her hands on her hips. "But did you look? Really look? You weren't up there very long, Barry Tate. Why don't you go back and look again?"

Brendan slanted a look at her. Was she angling to be left alone with him?

But Jenny sniffed. "This is boring. I don't think you're going to find that old violin anyway. Barry and I are going out for some drinks. Want to come?"

"Can't." Father Hurley would be arriving soon. Best to get everybody out of the house. Except Mary Grace. He wanted her to stay.

That thought floated in his mind even as he shooed Jenny and Barry out, leaving him and Mary Grace alone. Would he be mad to make a move on her now? Would she welcome it? Turn angry and accusing?

He didn't know, but the idea of taking her in his arms—of taking her back up to his room—went straight to his head. The physical part of their relationship always had been easy, as she said—instinctive.

He shut the door behind his fellow searchers and turned to find Mary Grace at his elbow, eyes dancing like two stars.

She whispered, "I have an idea."

So did Brendan, a whole horde of them spilling through his head. Had they time before Father Hurley arrived? He couldn't leave the priest standing outside the door while they pleasured one another.

Could he?

"Do you, darling?"

"Yup. Why don't you ask him?"

"Eh? Ask who, what?"

"The ghost, lummox. Before you exorcise him, of course."

"A brilliant notion." And had Brendan's brain not been clouded by lust, he might have thought of it. "That old reprobate must know where his fiddle is. The real

85

one, I mean—not the spiritual one he's been playing to torment me."

"Exactly." Mary Grace looked pleased with herself. "But he might not appear while I'm here, so I'd better go."

"No, Mary Grace, don't."

Her gaze, still welded to his, turned serious. "I think I should. Before I do something I'll regret."

"Would you regret kissing me?"

"Yes, oh, yes, I—"

He gave her time for no more. A gentle tug had her in his arms right up against his body, where she fit as if the last eight years had never happened. Brendan wrapped his arms around her, drew one breath of her scent, and dove for her lips.

Soft, warm with a flavor he'd never forgotten—they yielded to him with the same sweetness she'd always offered. Fiery, fierce, independent Mary Grace tended to melt at his touch like tallow to the flame, granting a piece of herself to him alone. Granting a haven, one that he could still find in her.

Oh, sweet Jesus and all the saints—one touch, one taste, and he was lost like a man overboard in rough seas.

He brushed his tongue against hers in an act of intimacy, explored the hot, delicious inside of her mouth with a long-remembered sense of claiming. Kissing Mary Grace had never been just kissing. How had he ever lived without this?

He broke the kiss to gasp raggedly in her ear, "Come to my room with me?"

Hours together, that's what he wanted, the two of them alone in his room, time aplenty to explore her body, taste her everywhere, and regain what had once been his. He wanted that so bad he could barely see straight.

But she whispered, "You sure that's not just the trifle talking?"

"No, it's you. I've missed you, Mary Grace, missed you so much."

"Out of the hundreds of girls you've had since we split?"

Now why would she bring up such a thing and spoil the moment? He answered truthfully, "None of them was you. There'll never be anyone else like you for me, Mary Grace."

She lifted her chin and stared into his eyes. What did he see in her gaze? A vast sea of emotions all teeming together. Desire, yes. God, yes. Anger, accusation—grief. Refusal. Damn it.

"Not a good idea, O'Rourke."

"I think it's one of the best ideas I've ever had." Maybe they could put their love back together again. Maybe she could help him put the pieces of his soul back together.

She shook her head. "What about Isolde?"

"What about her?" Brendan didn't want to begin all that again. He wanted to take this woman in his arms and make love to her till her eyes rolled back in her head and she gasped his name. "I can't make love to Isolde."

"You do, though. You do every time your fingers move over those strings."

"You're crazy, do you know that? You're jealous of a hunk of wood and some wire."

"Maybe I am. And that should be a warning to me.

87

Even though it would be the easiest thing to jump into bed with you…"

"You won't."

"I can't."

Rejection stung. Brendan drew himself up. "I don't think it's fair of you—I never thought it was fair—asking me to give up a part of myself just to be with you."

"I never asked that."

"You did. You wanted me to choose. But playing fiddle isn't just what I *do*. It's a big part of what I am."

"I know, and I never wanted you to give it up."

"Then—"

A knock sounded at the front door.

Mary Grace ignored it. "We're arguing again. I should have known. We can't be together without arguing."

"We can." If she'd just let him take her to bed. Damn it, he still wanted that even after she'd rejected him.

The pounding at the door sounded again.

"That will be Father Hurley. You don't want him to find me in your arms."

"No?"

"Let go of me, O'Rourke. I'm leaving."

"Don't you want to stay for the exorcism?"

"No. It was a mistake to come anywhere near you. You're poison."

"That's a hard thing to say, Mary Grace Dawe."

Father Hurley's voice called from outside. "Brendan O'Rourke, are you in?"

Mary Grace freed herself from Brendan's arms. "Where's my bag? Brendan, go open the door for the priest."

He followed her into the parlor, where she snatched up her purse from the table where she'd left it. As she walked past Brendan, she said, "Don't forget to ask Charlie about his fiddle before you banish him to the outer darkness. You still owe me a concert on Sunday. Brendan O'Rourke—you owe me."

Chapter Thirteen

"You're a fool, do you know it, Brendan O'Rourke? I'm that ashamed to admit you're my descendant."

Brendan glowered. He once more sat in the darkened kitchen with his heels propped on one of the chairs and a beer in his hand. No hope of sleep this night.

He glared at his great-grandfather. "Why are you still here after Father Hurley's exorcism?"

"Ah, bah." Charlie waved a hand. "That was no proper exorcism. The man just blessed the place with holy water. What's a wee bit of water, after all?"

"It was supposed to banish you. And yet I still find you"—Brendan waved his hand in turn—"hovering."

Charlie laughed heartily. "Didn't I tell you I was excommunicated years and years ago?"

"And that means you can't be banished?"

"The Church has no further influence over me."

"So an all-out exorcism wouldn't work either?"

"It would not."

Brendan contemplated that unhappily. "You might have made that a bit more clear before I committed myself to that fundraiser on Sunday. Now things are all stirred up with Mary Grace."

"And that brings us back to what a fool you are. During that clench upstairs…"

"You were watching?"

"Of course I was. And a pitiful performance, I might add."

"You're a fine one to throw stones, old man."

"I'm the very one to give you advice, hard learned from my own mistakes, so to speak. You had the woman there in your arms, steps from your bed. Why didn't you tell her whatever she wanted to hear?"

"I refuse to lie to Mary Grace."

"No?"

"I respect her too much for that."

Charlie made a rude sound. "Telling her what she wants to hear *is* respecting her, lad—and then living up to it as best you can. That's what a woman wants, and it's little enough for what they give us in return."

"She wants me to give up my music." Brendan's lip twisted. "After I play at her bloody fundraiser. How convoluted is that?"

"Convoluted as a woman's mind. But her heart, lad—oh, her heart is steady."

"You're wrong. She doesn't have feelings for me anymore. All that's gone. We just have this—this irresistible attraction between us. We always did. But the music's still between us also. Every time we're together, it comes up again and we argue."

"Doesn't still love you, eh?"

"No."

"Then why did she break it off with that poor sap she was supposed to marry?"

"That had nothing to do with me."

"Did it not?"

"I wasn't even here in St. John's when she broke it off with Chet. And we hadn't seen each other for—

well, years."

Charlie drawled, "So?"

"So," Brendan responded, surprised at how much this felt like talking to himself, "if she still had feelings for me, she never would have got engaged to him in the first place."

"Is that what you think? You just don't understand women at all."

"And I suppose you do?"

"A ghost hangs around a house through a couple marriages and he learns a good few things. Have I not just said what comes out of a woman's mouth doesn't always reflect what's in her heart? Especially when she's angry."

"Well, Mary Grace certainly has that covered. Say what you will, I believe what happened tonight was a result of an old attraction and that trifle."

"Well, of course it was." Charlie pointed a spectral finger. "And you failed to take advantage of it."

"All right, old man, what should I have told her?"

"That you realized, while pursuing your music hither and yon, you'd made a fatal mistake breaking it off with her. That you learned the hard way how terrible it is trying to exist without her. That her love is everything you need, and you'll worship at her feet if she'll just take you back again."

"I damn sure am not going to say any such thing. Why should I?"

"Because it's true."

"It is not. I've missed her, sure."

"Your heart is shattered."

"I suspect it's *your* heart we're talking about here. That may well be shattered. Get it through your transparent head—*I'm not you.*"

"You're after making the same mistakes I made."

"Maybe so. That doesn't mean you can live your life through me." Brendan scowled and waved his hand. "Why don't you go find your Bridget somewhere in the ether and make it up with her, if you want her so much?"

"I would if I could. I told you, she's gone where, for my sins, I can't follow."

"Well that's hard luck, and I'm sorry, but it doesn't mean I need to give up my music for Mary Grace. And it doesn't mean she gave up Hader because of me."

"Pig-headed, cloth-eared fool!"

"Pain in the arse!"

Silence fell in the dark kitchen, followed only by the sound of Brendan draining the beer bottle. "I'm going to bed. I trust you'll let me sleep?"

Charlie stretched his fingers and said rather nastily, "I think not. A wee bit of fiddle music's in order. Been far too long since I played."

Brendan snapped his fingers. "That reminds me—your fiddle. Is it somewhere in this house?"

A crafty look crossed the ghost's face. "Might be."

"Tell me where it's hidden. I need to borrow it, since mine got stolen."

"Isolde," Charlie sneered. "What kind of name is that for a fiddle?"

"I suppose yours didn't have a name."

"Of course she does. She's the lovely Guinevere."

Brendan groaned. "May I have permission to borrow and play Guinevere on Sunday? Presuming she's still playable, that is."

"She's in fine fettle. Why do you think I play so

much?"

"In order to drive me mad—and you haven't been playing an actual fiddle, have you? It's some sort of spectral one." Brendan paused. "All right, then, where is she?"

"I think I'll not tell you. Make you search."

"I have searched. I'll bet she's not here at all. I never heard tell of a fiddle hidden in this house."

"That's because no one knows the hiding place. Bridget put Guinevere away after I died. They brought the fiddle to her, and she protected it like the treasure it was."

Because she couldn't bear to look at it, more like.

"So tell me. Look, old man—I need it for Mary Grace's sake. So you'll be helping her, not me."

"In that case"—Charlie floated across the table, up to Brendan's ear—"listen."

****

Saturday afternoon, and Grace despaired as to whether everything would be ready before the event actually began the next day. As usually happened in such situations, chaos reigned supreme. Volunteers had showed up on the premise that many hands made light work, but all those hands needed directing, and everyone turned to her, Grace.

She had the vendors all set up near the parking lot, the beer tent erected, and various stations established at the museum buildings.

She paused and gazed out over the ocean, which she often did when she needed to center herself. At least tomorrow's weather promised to be good—perfect, in fact.

Now if only Isolde would turn up. No question

Brendan O'Rourke had become the main attraction and their biggest draw. If he didn't play, she couldn't guess what she'd do.

At that thought she glanced up and noticed Cabot coming toward her—with none other than Brendan O'Rourke at his side.

Her heart made that funny little stutter it always did when she saw him, the one that prophesied heart attack.

Once again he looked far too good, with his loose, long-legged stride, the air of casual confidence he wore like a coat, and the sunlight picking red lights from his hair.

She stiffened and pulled up her resistance, like donning armor.

"Afternoon, Brendan. I hope you have good news for me."

"I have." He grinned and hoisted a black case from his side, where Cabot's large furry form had concealed it. "Just look."

"They found Isolde?"

"It's not Isolde. It's Guinevere."

"I beg your pardon?"

He paused and stood looking down at her, the bright hazel gaze touching everywhere—her hair, her lips, her breasts.

"I got Charlie to cough up the information last night."

"Good work. Where was she?"

"Apparently, Bridget put her away behind a secret panel at the back of their closet, where they used to store other valuables."

"Anything else good in there?"

Brendan shook his head. "I suspect Bridget sold

everything else. There was just a small box with some trinkets."

"What kind of trinkets?"

"A dried flower, a lock of hair—that sort of thing. And a few letters."

"I'd love to see those."

Brendan said nothing—no invitation back to his house. After last time, could Grace blame him? She gulped a breath. "So what shape is Guinevere in?"

"Well, I had to replace her strings and spend quite a time tuning her, but see what you think."

He opened the battered, half-split case and whipped out the instrument. Placing it under his chin, he raised the bow, and the faraway look he always got when he played came to his eyes.

He laid bow to strings; fire ensued.

The fiddle, silent so many years, leaped to life. She chortled; she sang; notes danced from her, rose and twined through the air, spread over the rocks on the shore, and mingled with the water.

A slow chill chased its way down Grace's spine. What was she hearing? Music played by the man who stood in front of her or that played seventy years ago?

Brendan always played well. Now, with this fiddle in his hands, he wove magic, a plaintive, haunting tale full of tripping grace notes that brought tears to her eyes.

When the last note died away, lost in the hush-hush of the waves, they both stood perfectly still.

Brendan, emerging from his trance, rested his gaze on Grace's face.

"There, now, I did not mean to make you cry." He reached out a calloused thumb and brushed a tear from her cheek. "Mary Grace—"

I need to get hold of myself. I'm coming apart at the seams. It's just a song played on an ancient fiddle...

A song that revealed the beautiful soul of this man. How could I ever have wanted him to stop playing?

But I didn't, I didn't. I just wanted him to put it aside sometimes. For me.

"Don't be silly, why would I be crying? I'm just glad you'll be able to play tomorrow. So much is riding on it."

"I'll be here, Mary Grace. You can count on me."

Chapter Fourteen

The last guest had gone, and the last volunteer. Grace, still clad in her period costume, felt full to bursting with jubilant euphoria, despite her aching feet. She must have trotted twenty miles this day, covering the museum from one end to the other, doing her best to be everywhere at once.

Now, with the departure of Father Hurley—beside himself with the success of their takings—weariness descended all at once. The event had been scheduled to last till eight; it had run over and now dark rode on the ocean, beside which she and Cabot stood.

But oh, it had been a good day!

The big dog, tired out from being the center of attention, flopped down at her feet. Grace grinned at him and wished she could do the same.

She started when a door banged nearby—she'd been sure after Father Hurley left she and Cabot were alone.

But no, for someone came out of the saltbox house nearest the sea, whistling a tune. The song must have been one of the last he'd played, and it made a jaunty melody in the soft dark.

Brendan appeared, and Cabot wagged his tail lazily.

"I thought you'd gone," Grace said.

He shook his head, looking like little more than a

shadow. "I was talking with Father Hurley and then had to pack up."

"I didn't expect things to run so long."

He sounded pleased when he replied, "Always a good gig that goes long."

Grace couldn't help but smile. Brendan had invariably been energized rather than tired out when he played, no matter how long the session.

"I have to thank you, Brendan—you were a wild success. The definite hit of the event."

"I think the credit goes to Guinevere and my fellow musicians. The fiddle's magic, she is."

Grace had to agree. She'd stopped by the kitchen ceilidh several times to snatch a listen and found the other players struggling to keep up with the fire flashing from Brendan's bow.

He went on, "That doesn't mean I don't want Isolde back."

"They'll find her." On this night, Grace could believe in any sort of miracle, with that glorious dark settling onto the water, the houses of the museum gathered like a flock of sheep, lit only by the lights from the car park.

She could barely see Brendan's face, but oh, she could feel him—a potent presence in the dark.

"You must be weary," he said sympathetically. "Why don't you let me drive you home? You can pick up your car tomorrow."

"I planned to sleep here tonight." She gestured at the house behind them, the same in which he'd played. Visitors weren't allowed upstairs, but she had a bed there, along with the bare necessities.

"Sure that's wise, staying out here alone?"

"Not alone. I have Cabbie, here."

Brendan eyed the big dog wryly. "Cabbie appears to be asleep and likely to stay that way."

"I'll be fine, Brendan. Anyway, I'm not your responsibility."

"Are you not?" He set the battered fiddle case down carefully and stepped closer. "Funny that, because my heart feels differently."

"Your heart?"

"All this day long, the whole time I played, it was fixed on you, Mary Grace. I just couldn't get you out of my head. Every time you came in, I knew you were there."

Grace wanted desperately to deny that; she couldn't. She'd seen the way his gaze flew to her when she stopped by, how his attention—and his fingers—quickened.

"I wanted to talk to you, but I was always in the middle of a set."

"There's nothing left to talk about."

"Is there not?"

"No. I'm pretty sure we've said it all. And all that talking never got us anywhere."

"Maybe I need to stop talking, then."

Before Grace could react, he pulled her into his arms. The kiss started slowly, sweet as a gentle air skipped across fiddle strings, but almost instantly caught fire. Grace distinctly felt the heat leap from his blood to hers, and then she was lost, lost, lost without hope of salvation.

"Oh, God, oh, God," she whispered when his tongue finished sweeping her mouth and she rested, boneless, against him.

"My feelings for you aren't gone, Mary Grace. They never went away."

Neither had hers for him—deny it as she might. But she wouldn't lower her barriers and speak those words. She wouldn't, she wouldn't.

"Brendan, this is a mistake."

"I don't agree; I think it's one of the best ideas I've ever had."

Grace's heart agreed. Her mind struggled against the spell woven all around them, made from the music, his touch, and the darkness. He kissed her again, a kiss she felt all the way to her toes. This was what she remembered, what had made her forgive him again and again. This had made it so difficult to get him out of her blood.

But he spoke truly—she'd never really succeeded at that. She'd just fooled herself.

This time when the kiss broke they both breathed raggedly. He whispered into her ear, "Let me stay here with you tonight, Mary Grace."

No, no, no. A deadly mistake.

"Let's go inside and make up for all the time apart."

He was the devil whispering in her ear—pure temptation in the darkness.

"Really, really not a good idea." Because if she had him once how could she ever give him up again? Besides, not here—this place, the site of all her dreams, felt sacred and hers alone. If she let him in…

"No, Brendan. I dare not."

"Just the two of us, all night."

The words took Grace back. That had been her war cry in the days she felt she had to compete for every minute of his time. *Brendan, why can't it be just the two of us?*

Did he remember that? Or did he choose those words by chance?

She now knew she would never own this man, not even for one night. She'd be mad to go upstairs to the little room under the eaves with him, the place where she'd so often dreamed of him.

Yet the night beguiled her and the rhythm of her heart, and his hands that cradled her.

She could lie to herself again, pretend he was hers—touch him, taste him, give in to this terrible hunger that she'd endured so long.

And what about tomorrow? Her mind argued fiercely with her heart and her desire. *What then?*

She sought Brendan's eyes in the dim light, trying to read what truly lay there. Had he changed? Could he change? No fool she—she knew pinning her heart on that possibility would bring only hurt.

"What about tomorrow?" She asked it aloud.

"Eh?"

He'd not thought of that; of course he hadn't. Brendan rarely thought far ahead. To consequences, to things like children and old age. To *forever*.

"Tomorrow," she said desperately, "when I'll have to pick up the pieces of my heart."

He cupped her face between his hands. "Mary Grace," he murmured so sweetly her knees went weak, "trust me with your heart. *Trust me*."

She dared not. Yet now his fingers were in her hair, moving down her back, trailing fire. And her inner desire spoke more loudly, saying, *Just one night*, after all the loneliness and longing for him. What could it hurt—one night?

She sighed, and he took it for the answer it was. As if she weighed nothing, he swung her up into his arms, stooped to catch up the fiddle, and carried them both inside.

He kissed her just inside the door and again at the foot of the stairs. By the time they reached the top landing, Grace was lost, tumbled backward into a dream where this was their small house and he her husband, hers and no one else's, as had always been meant.

He carried her unerringly into the correct room— how did he know?—set the fiddle on the dresser, and moved with her to the bed, where he once more explored the inside of her mouth, taking his time with it.

By then she had her arms twined around his neck and her fingers buried in his hair.

Lost.

When he tried to place her on the bed, she refused to let go of him. He chuckled softly, an erotic sound in the dark room.

"Is there a light?"

"No light."

"But I'd like to see you, after this long wait."

"Brendan, don't ruin the spell."

"A spell, is it? All right."

"And don't let go of me," she breathed into the darkness. "Don't you dare let go."

Chapter Fifteen

So dreams do come true, Grace thought as Brendan drew the clothes from her body one garment at a time, chased by kisses. How many times had she cuddled by herself in this bed and imagined this very thing? The brush of his callused fingers against her skin, the scent of him, the rush of urgent desire that tumbled her head over heels.

All a woman needed to do in order to seize her dreams was risk everything… All the hard-won healing she'd achieved over the last eight years and her sanity. Who needed sanity? she asked herself as Brendan's tongue swept her mouth again, as they fought together to remove his shirt while maintaining lip contact. When, naked at last, his weight came down on her.

And after eight long years, her world suddenly snapped into place. This was what she'd wanted all this time. This.

And he knew. He'd always known just where and how to touch her to coax a maximum response. He knew she liked her kisses slow, accompanied by his fingers trailing down her side, at her breast, caressing her legs. Now he touched her everywhere, and the agony she'd carried so long eased.

"God, you're beautiful, Mary Grace. So beautiful."

She felt it, in his hands. She became a goddess when his mouth moved to her breast, when he worshipped her with his tongue.

"Feels so good," he gasped as he moved from one breast to the other.

"So good." She could barely speak for her desire. Heat roared through her as his clever fingers swept to the triangle of curls between her legs and sought admittance. She opened for him in a movement as primal as time and began to pray.

He abandoned her breast and returned his lips to her mouth where he whispered, "Tell me what you want, Mary Grace."

"Anything. Everything."

He laughed again, and her desire spiked impossibly. "I won't last long. Feel that?" He shifted between her legs.

"Yes." Hot and heavy.

"That's what you do to me."

"It's all right." She whispered like the madwoman she was. "We have all night."

"So we do." He invaded her with those long, graceful fingers.

"I'm about to explode. Too long, Brendan. It's been too long. Don't wait any longer."

"I won't. I can't." He laid his mouth on hers, claimed her with his tongue even as he nudged her thighs further apart and slid into her, the weight and heft of him fitting perfectly, as ever. They began to move together in a glorious dance there in the dark, their hearts in perfect rhythm, joined so completely Grace could no longer tell his desire from hers.

They climbed together and hung for one glorious moment before tumbling so quick and hard the world fell away. No past, no future—only Brendan.

Just as it had always been when he loved her.

Sanity returned slowly in pieces, and Grace tried to determine where and when she was. In the little room up in the saltbox. She'd left the window open earlier and could hear the *shush-shush* of the waves below. It came in time with Brendan's breaths that chased across the skin of her throat. He'd collapsed on top of her—a well-remembered and well-loved weight.

Well-loved? No, no, no. Not that. Oh, what had she done?

The one thing she could. Honesty washed through her in the wake of the lust, and she acknowledged the truth. She could no more resist this man than stop breathing. Even now the scent of him teased her, quickened her, and the soft tickle of his beard against her cheek.

Well, then—she couldn't undo what she'd just done. But how to protect herself moving forward?

They'd taken the edge off one another's need—she knew very well they weren't done. Should she allow herself the pleasure of a whole night with him? Just one night, and the damage already done...

Sex wasn't the problem; it never had been. What truly frightened Grace was the impulse she now had to tell him she loved him. She wanted to give him those words the way she'd just given him her body.

She absolutely could not.

He stirred and raised himself on his elbows. The soft hair on his chest brushed her overly-sensitized breasts, a delightful friction.

"Now I can take my time," he crooned, "and love you as you deserve."

Love me. But he didn't mean it, not the way she

did.

"But I want the light, Mary Grace. I want to see you, all of you."

"There's no electricity, just an oil lamp."

"Matches?"

"There—on the bedside table. For God's sake, don't knock the lamp over."

He moved away from her, and she bit back a protest. She heard him strike the match and lift the glass flue. Radiance flared golden and made her narrow her eyes.

Oh, and he made a sight to see with the mellow light flowing over his shoulders, throwing the planes of his face into relief, highlighting his hair, most of which stood on end. Had she done that?

A man from a dream; her dream. She'd never thought to have this again, and just looking at him made her throat close with emotion.

Just as well; she didn't want any words to slip out.

He smiled and her heart squeezed as if stabbed through.

"Look at you," he whispered. "Just lie there for me, in all your splendor."

He reared above her, resting on his knees atop the bed, contemplating the picture she made. Very gently he smoothed her hair on the pillow, spread her arms from her sides, traced the length of her legs with his palms. His gaze, hot as a torch, caressed both breasts. Grace's pulse accelerated helplessly.

"I've seen you this way a thousand times in my head," he whispered. "Just like this."

"You thought of me?" Grace's voice, husky, didn't sound like her own.

"Thought of you?" He closed his eyes like a man in pain. "What do you suppose?"

"I supposed you were happily jetting around the country, playing music and having a grand time."

"I was," he answered honestly. "But the real music—the first song—was always here with you, like this."

Grace wasn't sure she believed that. She didn't want to say so.

"I'm going to make love to you again, Mary Grace. And we're going to take it slow this time. You just lie there while I kiss you all over. I don't want to miss an inch."

"Brendan."

"And then, when I get done, it will be your turn."

Grace eyed him from the top of his head to the strong evidence of his desire jutting between his legs. Her mouth went dry. "Yes," she murmured. "Yes."

****

Brendan, surfacing briefly from the throes of passion, wondered if he'd died and gone to heaven. To be sure, heaven could be no better than this.

The lamp had burned up all the oil and guttered. Dawn, which came very early indeed at this time of year, had just begun to gray the sky. The smell of the sea came through the open window. Mary Grace Dawe lay in his arms, and the sweet taste of her still lingered on his lips.

What more could a man want? Nothing. There was nothing beyond this, fulfillment on a level so deep he could barely comprehend it.

Well, there was the music.

The thought trickled into his mind, carried in the

restless song of the ocean and in the rhythm of Mary Grace's breathing, even in the dance of the window curtains on the morning breeze.

He felt complete when he played the fiddle, as well; maybe not this complete, but it was damned close. Even now his fingers itched to pick up the instrument and play the way he'd played Mary Grace's lovely body.

God, how had he ever lived without her so long? And how was he going to keep her in his life without starting all the arguments again?

She still slept. Her lashes made two brown fans on her cheeks; her skin looked like alabaster. The rosy tips of both breasts pointed upwards, starting a potent longing inside him.

Last night she'd claimed a magic spell held them. Would it still hold this morning? If he woke her with caresses to those little roses, would she push him away?

Charlie's fiddle case lay on the dresser, where he'd set it when they came into the room. If he opened it and played a song, one that expressed all he felt for Mary Grace, would she know what it meant? Would she be able to tell it for his way of saying he loved her? Or would she just think he preferred the music over her, again?

He loved her. He'd never stopped. But nothing between them had changed—not the passion and, he feared, not the anger or doubt. So if he sat by the window and poured out his heart to her in a tune, she might not understand.

He dared not take the chance.

Despite all Charlie's advice, recommendations and warnings, Brendan suspected Mary Grace still felt he should be willing to give up his music for her. And he believed if she truly loved him she would not ask such a thing.

How to bridge that gap?

She stirred, and on impulse he caught her hand and planted a kiss in the palm. Her eyes came open—blue-gray and deep as the sea. Fathomless.

"Come on, Mary Grace, get dressed."

"What?"

"Hurry."

"Why?"

"We're going to see the sunrise."

"But—"

He drew her up by the hand and pulled her from the bed after him. Her hair fell in a wild tangle; she looked too beautiful for words.

He thrust her clothes at her. "I know I took these off, but I've no idea how they go back on. Just hurry."

"We'll never make it."

"Not all the way to the point maybe, but close enough. Mary Grace, I want to watch this day begin with you."

She gazed into his eyes, read what lay there, and nodded.

Not another word passed between them. Wearing no shoes, Brendan without a shirt and Grace with her bodice half open, they ran through the museum grounds, up the shore to a rocky outcrop which they reached, lungs heaving, just as the sun lifted over the sea.

Brendan pulled Mary Grace into his arms and held her tight. "There now," he crooned. "It's a new day. A new beginning, new for us."

She drew away far enough to look into his eyes. "New beginning?"

"No more anger, Mary Grace. Please."

"I don't think—"

"No words." And he kissed her, stealing them all.

Chapter Sixteen

"So you finally gained a lick of sense." Charlie hovered in the doorway of the kitchen, watching as Brendan set the table. "I'm glad to see it."

Brendan glanced at his great-grandfather. He had plans for tonight, and they didn't include Charlie. "If you're asking whether I've made things up with Mary Grace, I have. She's coming over tonight, and that means I don't need you here." He waved a hand. "Shoo."

"Is that any way to speak to your great-grandfather?" Charlie disappeared from the doorway and rematerialized floating over the end of the table, obviously tipsy. "The very man who orchestrated your reunion with the woman you love?"

"I thought I did that."

"Nonsense. I'm the one who talked you 'round. So, lad, did you tell her what she wanted to hear?"

"Not exactly. Our communication was more of the non-verbal variety."

Charlie got a big, sloppy grin. "I see. Swept her off her feet, did you?"

"Quite literally, yes."

"A woman likes that from time to time. I remember once me and my Bridget—"

"Pardon me, but your love life didn't end on a note that inspires confidence. I hope to do better."

"That's the spirit, lad! What's your plan?"

"Well, I've made supper. I have some wine. I'm going to get her in a mellow mood…"

"And then take her upstairs?"

"First I thought we'd attempt to talk about—things." Brendan's stomach did a somersault at the very thought. He wanted Mary Grace back. He didn't want to blow his chances by bringing up the past. But he felt some ground rules needed to be hashed out.

"Ah, bah!" Charlie cried. "Just take her upstairs."

"I'd like to, but if I do that, I'm afraid all the rest of it will just rear its ugly head once the passion dies down."

"But—"

"Either way, she doesn't need to find you here. So get."

Ignoring the order, Charlie floated over to the stove and peered at the covered pots. "What are you cooking? Doesn't smell like fish."

"You can smell food?" Brendan asked, momentarily diverted.

"Certainly, and other things. Sometimes I can still smell Bridget's perfume up in our bedroom. Lily o' the valley, it was."

"I didn't prepare any fish."

"Lord, lad, you should always feed a woman fish when you have romance in mind."

"I made pasta. Goes better with the wine."

"That's foreign cooking, is it? I don't approve."

"You don't need to approve or disapprove. I'm inviting you to leave."

"I think I'll hang about—invisible-like—and listen."

"No way. And I don't want you peeking later, if I get her upstairs."

"Fair enough. A man needs his privacy when making love to his woman. So what's it to be?"

"I beg your pardon?"

"These 'ground rules' you want to lay down. What are they? Will you tell her you're giving up the music?"

"No, I don't mean to lie to her. But it's like you said before: she needs to know she's important as well."

"Think you can manage having Mary Grace and the fiddle too?"

"God, I hope so." Brendan glanced at the kitchen clock and straightened the shirt he wore. "How do I look?"

"You're a handsome fellow and no mistake, though you could use a haircut. And do you call those proper trousers? Why don't you dress up a bit for her?"

"This from a man who died in the middle of the street, clutching a mug of ale."

"It was a bottle of whiskey, if you must know."

"Either way, it doesn't inspire sartorial confidence. And look at you now—neckcloth crooked, boots worn through—Is that what you were wearing when you died?"

"It is, to my sorrow. Bridget provided better clothes for the burial, but the undertaker's assistant stole them, so I was put in the ground like this. Never had a wake," Charlie added morosely. "Poor girl couldn't afford to buy the drink for one. So no one viewed me, anyway."

"Kind of ironic, isn't it? That after drinking yourself to death there'd be a lack of drink for a wake?"

Brendan was interrupted by a knock at the door.

"That will be Mary Grace. Now make yourself scarce."

He hurried to the door, stealing a last look back toward the kitchen and seeing the doorway empty. Thank God.

He hauled the door open, eager to see Mary Grace and gauge her mood. He found himself instead looking into the face of Johnny Rideout.

"What the hell?" Brendan cried.

Johnny's broad face wrinkled in a scowl. "A fine greeting. I hoped you might be just a bit happy to see me."

"I was expecting someone else."

"I've brought someone else." Johnny moved aside, and Brendan saw Johnny's girlfriend, Chrissy, perched on the stoop behind him. She gave Brendan a sickly smile.

"Surprise!"

"Ah, hell."

"Is that any way to greet us after we came all this way for a powwow? Aren't you going to ask us in?"

"I told you I'm—"

Brendan broke off as Mary Grace's car drew up at the curb. She climbed out and approached cautiously.

"Why, hello, Mary Grace," Johnny greeted her. "You're looking well. Are you two back together, then?"

"No," said Mary Grace.

"Yes," Brendan claimed at the same moment.

"Ah, well." Johnny lifted dark eyebrows. "Mary Grace, I'd like you to meet Chrissy Warkowski from Chicago. Chrissy, this is Mary Grace Dawe."

"Grace," Mary Grace corrected. "And of course you already know Brendan O'Rourke all too well."

Chrissy shot Brendan a dark look.

Mary Grace followed it with a questioning one. "Brendan, I didn't know you were expecting Johnny."

"He wasn't," Johnny answered. "I've come to see about getting the band started up again."

****

Grace poured herself another glass of wine even though she sure didn't need it. Supper, shared four ways rather than two, had been a disaster and not just because Brendan scorched the pasta sauce. It took Grace about two minutes to rediscover just why she'd never much liked Johnny Rideout.

How could she have forgotten what a bad influence the man was on Brendan? Johnny was the kind of fellow who liked to talk both sides of an argument and would push Brendan just for the hell of it. Not that she believed anyone but Brendan responsible for Brendan's choices, him being a grown man. But Johnny didn't help.

She spent the first hour wondering what Chrissy Warkowski saw in Johnny and the second wondering what Johnny saw in Chrissy. The woman had a laugh like a whinnying horse and seemed overly friendly.

Johnny laid it all out for them, saying he'd spent the last three weeks since the group disbanded convincing Chrissy what a tragedy it was and, quite frankly, talking her 'round. Then he turned to Grace and said, "Did Brendan tell you why we broke up?"

"Not exactly." Grace glanced at Brendan. "Why don't you tell me, Johnny?"

From the corner of her eye she caught Brendan waving his hands at Johnny urgently. To no avail. Once launched, Johnny was unstoppable.

"Chrissy here and I started a relationship, see, in Chicago. It got serious pretty quick, didn't it, lamb chop? But Brendan resented how much time I spent away from the band, and we started fighting over it."

Grace gave Brendan another sharp look.

"In my own defense, we hadn't had a rehearsal in a week. Johnny missed a show, and we had another big one coming, with new material to get battened down."

"I see," Grace said.

Chrissy leaned her elbows on the table. "It got so bad Brendan told Johnny to break up with me."

"I did not."

"What actually happened," Johnny put in, "was Brendan and I started bickering like an old married couple. At last he gave me an ultimatum."

"It wasn't an ultimatum," Brendan objected.

" 'Chrissy or the band' isn't an ultimatum?"

"I never said that."

"You told me I'd better get my priorities straight, that if I was going to spend that amount of time with a woman, we'd be better off scrapping the band."

Grace turned accusing eyes on Brendan, who shook his head.

"So," Johnny went on before Brendan could speak, "I chose Chrissy, as any right-thinking man would. We're in love."

"Why, certainly." Grace set her teeth.

"In fact"—Chrissy beamed—"we're going to have a baby. And"—she displayed her left hand, replete with diamond solitaire—"we're engaged."

"Jesus Christ," Brendan muttered, not quite under his breath.

"Congratulations," said Grace, feeling someone

should. "I'm pleased for you."

"So why are you here," Brendan demanded, "if you're set on playing happy families?"

"My Johnny's not happy," Chrissy said with a pout. "And I want him to be happy. If he needs the band for that, I'm all for it."

Brendan shot Grace a triumphant look. "No wonder you're in love with such a woman, Johnny, b'y."

"Hey," Chrissy said, "I knew the territory before I started dating him. I knew what it involved, and it wouldn't be fair of me to change the rules now."

"Besides, Brendan"—Johnny too leaned across the table—"we're tossing away our futures by disbanding. All the time and work we've put into building something good—can't just throw that down the crapper."

"So," Chrissy said sweetly, "I told him to come here and talk to you face to face, see if the two of you can work things out and get Kissin' the Cod started up again. There has to be some ground for compromise."

"Brendan's not a man for compromise, Chrissy," Johnny drawled. "Grace, here, can tell you that."

"I'm a perfectly reasonable man."

"Not when it comes to the music."

"All I said was there's no sense in us going out playing shows when we're unprepared. Talk about risking all we've worked so hard for—"

To Grace, Chrissy said, "He made me feel like Yoko Ono. But I'm no Yoko Ono; I'm willing to make sacrifices if it makes Johnny happy."

Grace heaved to her feet. "It's getting late. I'd better go."

Brendan rose also. "You've had quite a bit to drink, Mary Grace. I don't think you should drive."

"Well I'm certainly not staying here. I'll walk to Darcy's. That's just down the street. She'll put me up for the night."

She hurried to the front door; Brendan followed and caught her elbow before she could slip out.

"Mary Grace, wait." She could see the frustration in his eyes. "I didn't expect them to turn up. Johnny never so much as called me."

"Probably because he knew you'd refuse to see him. Is it true, Brendan? Did you break up the band because he fell in love?"

"No. He's the one who broke up the band."

She looked him in the eye. "Did you give him an ultimatum?"

"No. Yes. It wasn't the way he makes it sound."

"You tell me, how was it?"

He gestured wildly. "Just like I told you back in there—I asked him to sort out his priorities. I think that's reasonable. We all have a lot invested in this."

"So Kissin' the Cod is your top priority? The end all and be all?"

"I'm not saying that either. But Johnny should have considered—"

"Brendan, she's carrying his child."

"That doesn't change the fact that—"

"Doesn't it?" Grace interrupted him again. She lowered her voice to a snarl. "And if I were carrying your child? If I am? In case you've forgotten, you neglected to use a condom last night."

He paled. "Oh, hell."

Anger and hurt pounded through Grace in equal

measures. "I'm leaving. And don't call me. Don't try and see me again. It's over, understand?"

She didn't slam the door on the way out. A woman had to retain some dignity.

Chapter Seventeen

"So, lad, it seems you truly are following in my footsteps. Not necessarily a good thing, is it? Did you not heed my warning?"

Brendan looked up moodily from the beer bottle on the table. Three a.m. and he'd had no sleep, no hope of any. Awake again on Garland Street.

Upstairs in the guest room, Johnny and Chrissy slept, presumably. Johnny had hinted how much better it would be for them to stay here than at a hotel, and under the impetus of hospitality Brendan felt he had no choice but to agree, even though it was the last thing he wanted.

Now he advised sourly, "Go away, old man. Haven't you done enough?"

Charlie widened his eyes. "Me? What have I done? I've gone out of my way to make things right between you and the lovely Mary Grace, even as I cannot with my Bridget. I chased away that loose woman you brought home from the bar, the one who stole your fiddle."

"She wouldn't have stolen Isolde if you hadn't terrified her."

"That is an untruth. I have done all I could to arrange for you and Mary Grace to be alone together. Do you appreciate it?"

"No."

"Ungrateful as well as a chip off the old block."

"Listen, I'm not all that much like you."

"No? I cared more for my interests than for the welfare of my wife and son. Now you say you care for Mary Grace—"

"I do."

"But not more than you care for yourself. What if she does bear your child?"

Brendan stared, aghast. "You're not saying you know something, are you? With your ghostly powers?"

Charlie waved his hands mysteriously. "And if I do?"

"Can you tell these things?"

"I cannot. But for the sake of argument, I tell you, lad, don't take such a gamble. If there's any chance, go down on your bended knee and beg her forgiveness as I can no longer beg my Bridget's. Otherwise you'll live—and die—to regret it."

"Damned if I will. Why do women get their claws in a man and then decide they have the right to tell him what to do? That Chrissy, now…"

"A fine-looking woman."

"You think so? I would have said otherwise. Johnny's dated hundreds of women over the years."

"Just like you."

"Many of them prettier and certainly sweeter-natured than this one. Why her? Why jump when she snaps her fingers and start letting her run his life, especially when there's so much at stake?"

"Well," Charlie offered, "this Chrissy does have huge—" He cupped spectral hands in front of his own chest.

"That doesn't mean anything. There are plenty of

women with big breasts. Anyway, breasts are no reason for a man to toss all his common sense out the window. Do you know she set up a calendar for him, back in Chicago? He was allowed to rehearse when she said so, which basically boiled down to when she had nothing else scheduled for him. I just don't get it. Out of all the accommodating women, why her?"

"Well, lad, breasts aside, there's no accounting for love. It just swoops down on a fella like a hawk on a dove." Charlie grinned. "Did you hear that? I made a rhyme then."

Brendan eyed his great-grandfather with disfavor. "You're drunk again."

"I'm drunk still. We've already established it's now a permanent state."

"Why should I listen to the advice of a drunkard?"

"Because I have your best interest at heart. If I can't save myself, I'm determined at least to save you."

"Why not just leave me be?"

"I've no wish to watch me own flesh and blood suffer the way I have."

"Then don't watch."

A moody silence fell. Charlie hovered in the air, and Brendan stared at his near-empty bottle.

After a while, Charlie asked in a wheedling tone, "Did I ever tell you how I met my Bridget?"

Brendan shook his head.

"We met in Church."

That made Brendan look up, startled. "What the hell were you doing in Church?"

"Well, I'll tell you. It was springtime, and Father Muldoon was after having a special ceremony to bless the animals. He planned a little fete after, and he got some of the boys in to play at it—pretty music, he said." Charlie wrinkled his nose. "One of the lads dragged me in to play the fiddle."

"Weren't you afraid to walk through the door, in case the roof fell in on you?"

"I did not intend to go inside—just play the music in the yard, after Mass. But a load of ducks got loose."

"Ducks?"

"And then some hens. Everyone started chasing them around inside the Church. It looked like great fun."

"That's your idea of fun, is it?"

"It was. A bevy of lovely young women all squealing and kicking up their heels so you could see their petticoats."

"Oh."

"And then, in between the pews, I came face to face with Bridget McEwan. We were both after the same hen. Ah, lad—she had a face full of laughter, and she looked pretty as the spring day outside."

Brendan said nothing. Mary Grace, too, looked beautiful when she laughed. He felt a tug at his heart.

"I was struck. Struck," Charlie went on, "just as if somebody hit me on the head with a cudgel. That merry, fair face all flushed, and eyes of blue, she had. Hair like red Irish gold. You ask why, Brendan—why her? How can I tell? I'd consorted with a lot of women down the taverns and on the waterfront. None could touch her. I swear, a man just *knows*."

Brendan's stomach turned over in a slow roll. "So how did you get past the capture of the hens—you such a sinner and her a good Irish Catholic girl?"

"Well, I kept my eye on her at the fete, and I could

not help noticing she kept her eye on me. I played my best, most of the tunes just for her. When I played "The Star of the County Down," I never looked away from her. She brought me something to drink between sets, with her lovely, narrow hands..."

"Not ale, I'll warrant."

"No. And I looked into her beautiful face and asked if she'd walk out with me the next day, and the next and the next. I asked her if she'd walk out with me forever."

"And she agreed?"

"She did. She even defied her family for my sake. Her father didn't like me."

"I wonder why?"

"But he died soon after, trampled by a runaway horse on Water Street."

"A lot of animals run amok in this story."

"After that, her ma—a meek sort of woman—didn't object so much when I came calling. Bridget was the only child left home, see. And her ma soon went to live with her sister in Carbonear. I convinced Bridget then it would be a good idea to marry me."

Charlie hesitated, a confounded look on his face. "We were married there in that same Church. And I made promises that day which I failed to keep."

"How'd you wind up with this house?"

"It had belonged to Bridget's grandfather—the only thing she inherited from him."

"So." Brendan hated to ask. "How long before things began to come apart at the seams?"

"Not long. My living, see, was where the music got played—I had to earn pay for Bridget, but that took me to taverns and worse places. I couldn't leave the music alone, nor the drink, if I'm honest. Even though she asked me—even though she begged."

Brendan stared in horror as two big, ghostly tears ran down Charlie's face. "And all the while, 'twas I who should have been on my knees to that blessed woman. Just as you should kneel now to Mary Grace Dawe."

Brendan snorted. "I don't think so."

"Lad, your pride makes a cold companion for eternity."

"It has nothing to do with pride. She won't see me. Won't speak to me. I've nowhere to kneel, even if I wanted to."

"And do you want to?"

Brendan thought about that. "No. But…I might be willing."

"Ah, a bit o' sense at last! Can you not call her on that magic wee box of yours?" Charlie nodded at the cell phone that lay on the table.

"I tried. She doesn't answer. If I keep it up, she'll have me arrested for stalking."

"Nonsense. The lass loves you. Go see her in person. You know where she lives?"

"Well, of course I do."

"Take yourself there. Kneel down…"

"Not so much with the kneeling!"

"It's effective, lad. What woman can resist an earnest man on his knees? Especially when she loves him."

"You keep saying that, but I'm not so sure Mary Grace does love me."

"Of course she does, you half-wit. Why do you suppose she's so hurt?"

"The last thing I want to do is hurt her. Maybe I'm better staying away. Anyhow, what if I go there and she refuses to open the door?"

"Go see her at that museum place—the site of your grand passion."

"Hmm." Brendan's heart quickened.

"She cannot lock the door there, can she, lad?"

She couldn't. But should Brendan take the advice of an intoxicated spirit?

Chapter Eighteen

"Did you hear?" Darcy Butler asked as Grace searched through a pile of purchase orders. "Kissin' the Cod got back together. The other two band members flew in to St. John's yesterday and they're all supposed to play tomorrow at Fitzgerald's, to celebrate."

Grace froze where she stood, her hands full of papers. "You're kidding."

She hadn't spoken with Brendan in the last week, though she had to admit, not for lack of trying on his part. He'd called her a dozen times, calls she'd let go to voicemail where his messages, increasingly desperate, decreased to no message at all. She even thought she'd glimpsed him a couple of times here at the museum, once when she was conducting a tour, always at a distance. But they'd not met face to face.

"Yes," Darcy went on eagerly, "Billy told me. He talked to Brendan, who said they'll be letting local musicians sit in with them—he invited Billy to share a session with him again. Billy's ever so excited."

Well, that was that, then, Grace thought, and a tiny, lingering bit of hope she hadn't known existed died. She must have secretly imagined, with the breakup of the band, Brendan O'Rourke might settle down—not give up music, no, she'd never expect that. Music was part of Brendan, maybe the truest part. But he might have rooted himself here in St. John's, started a solo career. God knew he had the talent.

She thought of how his fingers played the fiddle—how they'd played her body that night they'd spent together after the fundraiser, and shivered as if she had fever.

That was just sex. Nothing on which to pin a future.

"You going to come and hear them play?" Darcy asked innocently, unaware she'd just blown a hole in Grace's lifeboat. "I imagine the place will be packed. But he'll make room for you."

Would he? Was there any room for her now that his other band members had returned?

St. John's boys all; the group had started here, playing in places like Fitzgerald's, had gained force and fame that spread beyond the boundaries of both Newfoundland and Canada. Their first album had been a smash hit. Grace had it at home but couldn't stand to play it. Not ever.

"When did you say this wondrous performance will take place?"

"Tomorrow night."

"I think I'm busy tomorrow night, Darcy."

"You can't be!"

"I am." She wasn't about to follow Brendan O'Rourke around like a groupie or watch other women fawn on him.

"Well, better change your plans. This is going to be the event of the year. Besides, they're hometown boys. We need to support them."

And how long before the band, reunited, tired of the local scene and returned to Chicago, where they'd been based for some time? Or went touring? He'd be gone from her life just as swiftly as he'd appeared.

Her misfortune that she still wanted him, ached to touch him, breathe his scent and hear him laugh in the darkness. Too bad for her she'd given in to him that one night, reigniting the fire.

Fool, fool, fool. Couldn't she take a hint from poor Bridget O'Rourke's fate? Left alone and penniless—with a child, no less.

Take a warning, girl. Keep away from him.

Easier said than done.

"I think," Darcy went on, "you should go in there tomorrow dressed to the gills and knock him dead." She gestured at Grace's costume. "Lose those fuddy-duddy clothes, put on that red dress of yours and some four-inch heels. You're stunning when you dress up."

Grace could do that. She might just sink so low, and put herself on display for him.

"As if he'd care," she said aloud.

"He'd care. I saw the way he looked at you here that day. And," Darcy added, "the way you looked at him."

"I did not."

"I thought you were going to eat him alive."

A tantalizing thought. But she'd already established, in her mind, sex was just sex.

Too bad she couldn't convince her body of that.

"Let me think about it," she said, just to get Darcy to quit pestering. "See if I can free up some time."

"You'll be sorry if you don't."

Three hours later, Grace was conducting a tour for a small group of visitors that included a charming Japanese couple, who'd already visited Gros Morne and Lanse aux Meadows, when she caught a glimpse of movement from the corner of one eye.

She paused in the middle of explaining the purpose of the fish stages and saw Brendan O'Rourke once more approaching, with Cabbie at his side.

Traitorous dog.

Her heart sped up and heat flushed her skin. Nowhere to hide. But surely he could see she was occupied? If she stalled and drew out the tour, maybe he'd go away.

He didn't. He sat on the rocks while she answered questions and dawdled over her answers, and waited patiently while her group fussed over the big dog. When she escorted them back to the souvenir shop where the tours ended, he trailed them, his hands in his pockets, moving in that tall, loose-limbed way he had— the one that fired her blood.

It looked like she'd have to talk to him. *Caught, girl. Just keep your head.*

She said goodbye to her tourists and looked around futilely for another group before turning to him.

"Hello, Brendan."

"Mary Grace." Hands still shoved in his pockets, he inspected her slowly from her hair downward, lingering a little too long on her lips.

"Something I can do for you?"

He hesitated, and his gaze, wide and hazel in the clear afternoon light, returned to her eyes. What did she see there? Far too many emotions to distinguish only one.

"You've been avoiding me and refusing my calls. Why?"

And there it was, the question. She supposed she owed him the truth. "I couldn't face it," she admitted, "couldn't bear going through all that again."

" 'All that'?"

"You know."

"I do not."

"Come on, Brendan. You may be a lot of things; you're not stupid."

"Well, that's encouraging. For all my multudinous flaws, a lack of brain isn't one of them. Is that it?"

"Or a lack of charm. Or willingness to change."

"That again, eh?"

"That *still*. Brendan, the tune never changes. Don't you get that?"

His face closed down tight. "I thought something had finally changed. That night we spent here—"

"Was great, yes, sure."

"—was significant."

Her gaze flew to his again. "But obviously not. Your reaction to Johnny and Chrissy proved abundantly you still think relationships should be relegated to the background, way behind the band."

"God damn it to hell, Mary Grace! The problem I had with Johnny back in Chicago had to do with him, not his relationship with Chrissy. Why does nobody seem to see that?"

She squared her stance. "Let's look at that, shall we? Just what exactly was your problem with Johnny?"

"His level of commitment. Success like we've achieved doesn't just happen. We've worked long and hard. Made sacrifices. God knows, I did."

"You did?"

"What do you think? Now who's being stupid? Leaving you here in St. John's was the hardest thing I've ever done. And he risks throwing it away for some empty-headed bimbo of a woman with big breasts." He waved a hand wildly. "There are thousands of women in the world with big breasts, and half of them want Johnny Rideout."

"The other half want Brendan O'Rourke?"

"That's not the point. The point is it's not like she's anything special. It's not like she's *you*."

Grace drew a breath that scorched her lungs. "Listen, we can't stand here in the car park, yelling. This is no place—"

"We need to talk, damn it. We're going to hash it out. I finally tracked you down, and it's time."

"I'm working, Brendan."

"When are you done?"

"The museum closes at six."

"I'll wait."

"Brendan," she said desperately, "we'll just argue. It's never done any good to talk."

"It will this time." A muscle jumped in his cheek.

"All right. Go sit by the water. I'll join you as soon as I can."

****

By the time Mary Grace joined Brendan in his seat above the stages, the beautiful, sunny day had begun to fade. A bank of fog moved in over the water, materializing much the way Charlie did in the kitchen.

Brendan spared a thought for his great-grandfather as Mary Grace slipped onto the rock beside him.

Wish me luck, old man. For he sensed he'd get one chance—no more—to tell Mary Grace all he must.

"Well, now," he said softly, his voice echoing over the water. "Is everyone gone?"

"Yes." She didn't look at him but watched the fog

bank, her profile and her shoulders rigid. Would she even listen?

"Why wouldn't you take my calls, Mary Grace? Don't you owe me that much?"

"Owe you?" She did look at him then, eyes wide and filled not with anger, as he expected, but sorrow.

That hit him in the gut, that he could be the cause of that look in her eyes. The last thing he'd ever wanted was to make her unhappy. Yet it seemed to happen over and over.

"Yes," he told her. "I think we do owe each other some honesty and respect, if we're in a relationship."

"We aren't," she said starkly. "All that ended long ago."

"Did it?"

"Yes, oh yes."

"The other night—"

"The other night"—she spoke carefully now, as if she'd rehearsed the words—"was just sex."

"Just sex?"

"An aberrant action on my part. A slip of my sanity, an hour of madness, but just sex all the same."

"Mind-blowing, earth-rattling sex."

"I didn't say it wasn't. But one night of disaster does not a relationship make."

"Disaster? That's what you think of me, Mary Grace?"

"It's what I think of us."

"I see." Now he stared out over the water, unable to face what he saw in her eyes. Well, he'd wanted honesty, hadn't he?

"It's done, Brendan. Let it be done. Go back to your band and your fame and your life, and forget about me."

"That's just it, Mary Grace. I don't think it's done for me. I still have feelings for you. They never went away."

"I still have feelings for you too, obviously. I suppose I always will. But if you want the complete truth—"

"I do, yes. That's why I'm here."

"I don't think I can do that again, go through that again."

"So you said before. What, precisely, is 'that'?"

"The struggling and the wondering, trying to sublimate my feelings. The coming in second to the band."

"What about the love? You're saying that's not worth making some adjustments, some sacrifices?"

"It's not love, Brendan. And it's not worth it if all the sacrifices are on one side."

He got to his feet, surging up all in one movement, so filled with anger and grief he thought his heart would burst. "Not love?" He threw the words at her. "You trying to tell me how I feel for you?"

She stumbled up also and teetered on the rock. "No. I'm telling you how I feel for you."

He reeled with it, just as if she'd delivered a blow across his face.

There you go, fool. She can't put it any clearer than that. So why are you still standing here?

"I see. I see at last, Mary Grace. Thank you."

He stomped off, and never saw the tears in her eyes.

Chapter Nineteen

"Don't you think you're going a bit heavy on the booze, b'y?" Ned Stokey rested his accordion on his knee and dropped the words in Brendan's ear. "Any more, and you'll start tripping over those strings."

Brendan glared at his fellow band member. Fitzgerald's was rocking, packed to the gills, and had been for the past four hours, everyone having a grand time.

Everyone, that was, except Brendan.

"Are you sayin' my playing's not up to snuff?"

"No, never that. But I do believe you're drunk."

Was he? Well and so what, as long as it didn't affect his playing. Hadn't Charlie played drunk most the time?

And did he really want to model his life on Charlie's?

"It's just," Ned pressed, "you usually drink ale between sets, not whiskey."

"It's a whiskey kind of night." Brendan had spent the first half of it watching the door, hoping Mary Grace would come in and the second half despising himself for it.

Of course she wouldn't show. She'd told him quite plainly what she thought of him, of them. She'd never show her face now.

Just sex? If that had been just sex, he was a six-fingered monkey. *Maybe just sex to her, b'y. You did such a fine job of chasing her away eight years ago, she'll not risk her heart again.*

Maybe Charlie had been right; he should have gone down on his knees. Too late now. He wouldn't get the chance.

"What the hell's with you tonight, anyway?" Ned asked. "You've a face like a slapped backside. Just go easy on the drink, will you?"

"Why should I? I can walk home from here."

Chrissy came pushing in then, elbowing her way through the crowd with a black ale in either hand. She handed one to Johnny and one to Brendan.

"Don't do that," Ned objected. "He's drinking whiskey."

"What's that? Can't hear." Chrissy beamed. "Do you believe this place? Oh, I love this town!"

Ned groaned. Rory Sullivan leaned in from behind, his bodhran still in his hands. "Hey, O'Rourke, should you be drinking that? You're already—"

"What the hell?" Brendan turned on him. "You think I can't play with a skinful? Just listen to this."

He lurched to his feet and raised Charlie's battered old fiddle. At the first drag of the bow across the strings, the bar went silent. Everyone there just knew this was a moment.

Later, folks all over St. John's would talk about it: Were you there? Were you at Fitzgerald's the night Brendan O'Rourke caught his bow on fire? Have you ever heard anybody fiddle so fast? Did you ever hear such playing—a thing of pure beauty, by God!

He played for nearly ten minutes straight, and nary a wrong note. All the while he kept thinking, At least I still have the music.

****

"Let's get him home. You take one arm, and I'll take the other. Mind the fiddle, now. He'll kill us if anything happens to that."

"This is just embarrassing. Good thing most the patrons have gone."

Brendan heard the voices conversing over his head, but dimly. Johnny and Rory were speaking to one another.

Ned chimed in. "I tried to warn him. He was going awfully hard on the Irish. Heave him up, now."

"If you're taking him home, be sure and put a bucket next to his bed. Johnny, honey, do you think we should stay there with him tonight?"

That was right; Johnny and Chrissy had moved to a downtown hotel when Rory and Ned arrived. He had the house to himself again—him and Charlie. Two of a kind.

His friends heaved him up, one beneath each armpit. His stomach teetered on the verge of losing its contents.

"This isn't like him," Rory declared. "Should we be worried? I mean, he is the heart of the band."

"I beg your pardon?" Johnny flared with mock outrage.

"No worries," Ned put in. "Did you hear him play? Did you ever hear the like? Even with a skinful."

"Take him home," Chrissy called, "and be sure to make him drink some water."

They stumbled out into the night. The air had cooled, and a thousand stars arched overhead. Brendan could smell salt on the wind.

It turned his stomach.

"Maybe I should stay with him," Rory declared as they humped him down George Street toward home.

"All right, b'y, you do that. Call us if you have any problems."

"Problems? What sort of problems would I have?"

"He says the house is haunted."

Rory swore bitterly. "I'm not staying there, then."

"He'll be fine on his own. Some water, a bucket—let him sleep it off."

At the door they searched Brendan's person for his keys and found them, with some difficulty. They dragged him and Guinevere inside.

"The bed or the chesterfield?"

"Chesterfield. I'm not dragging this big ox up all them stairs."

Good friends, Brendan thought. They settled him in the parlor with a glass of water and a wastepaper basket. Then they went crashing out, and silence settled around him.

Brendan lay aching, his head going around slowly—or was that the room?—and his stomach in revolt. He eyed the wastepaper basket and thought about dying.

"Well, and aren't you a pitiful sight."

He gulped as Charlie materialized and floated over the coffee table.

"Go away," he said weakly.

"Your friends have all deserted you. That doesn't mean I will. How about a tune?" Charlie whipped out a ghostly replication of Guinevere and set bow to strings.

"No. Please, God, no."

"What's that, lad?"

"Sleep. Can't you let me sleep?"

"No, I can't. You might expire. Don't you know I was no drunker than you the night I fell down and died?"

"Let me die, then."

"By Saint Patrick's beard, I'm ashamed to call you my descendant. What kind of attitude is that? On your feet, lad. Faint heart never won fair lady."

"The fair lady doesn't want me."

"The hell she don't! You're bound to miss your chance, and I'll be damned if I'll let you end up the same way I did." Charlie stared Brendan in the eye. "So get up and go woo the lady. Or would you rather I played for you all night?"

****

Brendan reeled down Mary Grace's street beneath the dancing stars. Or were they standing still? He breathed the cool air, sucked it deep into his lungs, before stumbling into the lobby of the apartment building where he knew Mary Grace lived. He tripped up the half dozen steps, found her door, and rapped loudly.

He hoped she wasn't asleep. It must be very late, so he pounded harder and called her name. "Mary Grace! Mary Grace Dawe!"

The door opened so abruptly Brendan, who leaned on it, almost fell down. A man stood there in a pair of pajama bottoms with all his hair on end.

"Who the hell are you?" Brendan demanded.

"Henry Cavendish."

"What are you doing in Mary Grace's apartment?"

"This isn't Mary Grace's apartment, b'y. She's next door."

"Oh. I'm very sorry."

Cavendish shut the door, and Brendan stumbled to the next portal, where he resumed his assault.

"Mary Grace! Open the door, darlin'!"

It opened swiftly. Mary Grace stood there in a sleep shirt, her brown hair streaming down. "For God's sake, Brendan, what are you doing? It's the middle of the night."

"I am fully aware of that."

"And you're drunk."

"I believe that point is irrelevant. I'm here to woo you."

She stared at him the way she might look at Charlie if he appeared in front of her. Clearly just arisen from her bed, she looked good, damned good, the thin fabric of the nightshirt caressing all her curves. A sight to bring a man to his knees, all right.

So Brendan knelt down in the hallway at her feet.

"Mary Grace Dawe, I've come to say I love you."

She goggled at him in horror—scarcely the reaction he aimed to provoke. Her lips parted but not a sound emerged.

Cavendish's door opened back up, as did the door across from Mary Grace's.

"Grace," Cavendish began.

"Do you mind? This is private."

"If it's private, take it inside. Do you know what time it is?"

The woman in the doorway across the hall, elderly and white-haired, objected, "No, don't make them go in. He's very handsome, isn't he? Is he going to ask her to marry him?"

Cavendish shrugged.

"He is not," Mary Grace said. "He's just drunk." She yanked at Brendan's shirt. "Get up, for God's sake."

He stared up at her sullenly. "I thought a woman liked a man on his knees."

"Oh, she does," the elderly lady sighed.

"Brendan, go home."

"I don't think I'll make it that far, to be perfectly honest."

"Well, how did you get here?"

"I walked."

"Better take him inside, girl," Cavendish advised.

"Goodness, yes," breathed the elderly lady. "You've no choice but to keep him all night."

Brendan climbed to his feet and gave Mary Grace a crooked grin. "Are you taking me inside?"

"Oh, for goodness' sake, come on."

Chapter Twenty

"You're a pitiful specimen, Brendan O'Rourke."

"That's what Charlie said."

"I've never seen you this drunk. You don't do drunk. The most I've ever seen you is loosened up on the ale."

He leaned toward her and confided, "I've been drinking Irish whiskey."

"Why? What happened at Fitzgerald's tonight?"

"Nothing. Absolutely nothing. You didn't come."

"Did you really expect me to?"

"I hoped." He clutched his chest dramatically. "Hope, apparently, really does spring eternal. Ah, but you should have heard me play! I've never played so well. At least I still have my music, even if you don't want me."

"I never said I didn't want you, Brendan." Grace blew out a breath. "Sit down on the chesterfield. Don't move a muscle till I bring you a bucket. I don't want you throwing up on my floor."

"All right. Your neighbors are very nice, aren't they?"

"Yes."

"They thought I was going to propose to you. Do you want me to propose to you?"

Grace, halfway back from the kitchen with the mop bucket in her hands, froze. "Not in this condition."

"Or at all?"

"I didn't say that either." Grace frowned at the man she loved. In the dim room, illuminated only by the ambient light from the hallway, he looked bleary-eyed and messy-haired.

"You said what we had wasn't love because all the sacrifice was on one side. Is that so?"

"It is."

He raised his hands—those beautiful, talented hands. "So tell me how to make things right."

At last he asked the question, the one she'd awaited so many years, and he had to be in this condition to get to it. Despair touched Grace's heart. "I told you I don't want to do this anymore. I can't bear to do this anymore."

"Do you want me back on my knees?"

"No."

"Isn't it true, what Charlie said? That no woman can resist a man on his knees?"

"It's difficult, but I think I can manage to resist."

"Then, Mary Grace, light of my life, what do you want me to do?"

"Stop coming over all Irish on me, for one thing. Sleep off this load you've supped."

"We'll talk in the morning?"

"Yes, probably. You sit still there while I make up a bed for you."

"I'm not sleeping with you?"

"You are not."

"Well, at least give us a kiss." He leaned toward her.

She planted a hand in the center of his chest. "I won't, Brendan O'Rourke. You stink."

"Damn it," he said. "Charlie was wrong. That's the last time I take the advice of a drunken ghost."

****

By noon the next day it was all over town that Brendan O'Rourke had asked Mary Grace Dawe to marry him.

Grace, who'd roused a groggy Brendan at nine a.m. and thrown him out of her apartment in an effort to make it to work on time, first heard the news when Darcy came to her, round-eyed.

"Why didn't you tell me?"

"Eh?"

"I thought we were friends."

"We are friends, Darcy."

"Funny, then, I should find out through the gossip mill."

Grace sighed. Her head hurt as if she'd been the one drinking last night.

"If you wanted to keep it a secret," Darcy persisted, "the cat's already out of the bag."

"Keep what a secret?"

"That you and Brendan O'Rourke are engaged."

Grace sprang to her feet. "Where did you hear such a thing?"

"From Billy, who just stopped by. But like I say, it's all over St. John's. Big news, this."

"False news."

"But they're saying he came to your door in the middle of the night and went down on one knee."

"Mrs. Senet," Grace hissed. "She must have talked about what she saw."

"That old woman? She's a terrible gossip." Darcy's eyes grew round. "Why, what did she see?"

"He did come to my door last night, but he wasn't down on one knee." It had been both knees. "And he didn't ask me to marry him." He might have, but who wanted a drunken proposal of marriage?

Anyway, did she want to marry Brendan O'Rourke? She had, once. There'd been a time when she couldn't imagine doing anything else.

Things changed, she told herself firmly. And Brendan hadn't.

"This is awful. All over town, you say?"

"According to Billy."

"Brendan will have to set things straight. This is all his fault."

"Oh. I'm so disappointed. I hoped you'd have the wedding here in St. John's."

"Just shows you, you shouldn't listen to rumors."

****

"You sly dog!" Johnny's grin looked twice as wide as his face. Behind him stood Chrissy, holding a bunch of flowers.

"Eh?" Brendan stared out from the doorway blearily. "What time is it?" He'd fallen back asleep after Mary Grace sent him home, and now his head felt like she'd cleaved it with an axe.

"After noon. Let us in, b'y. We need to celebrate."

Brendan stepped aside reluctantly. "Celebrate what?"

"Ah, just listen to him," Johnny said to Chrissy as they charged in. "And after all the grief he gave us."

"Now Johnny, honey, be charitable." Chrissy glanced around. "Is Grace here? I brought her some flowers."

"Mary Grace, here? Why would she be here?"

"Well, you should be celebrating, newly engaged and all." Chrissy shot a sly look at Johnny. "Remember how we celebrated, honey, when you proposed to me? Two days in bed."

"Right," Johnny said blithely. "I only got up to piss."

"What's that?" Brendan blinked at him.

"Well, old son, a man has to relieve himself."

"Not that. Engaged. You said 'engaged.' I'm not engaged."

"That's not the word on the street."

Brendan swallowed spasmodically. What had happened at Mary Grace's apartment last night? He knew he'd gone there at Charlie's urging. He knew he'd spent most of the night there. Everything else remained pretty foggy.

Had he asked Mary Grace to marry him? Had she said yes?

His heart quivered in his chest, torn between hope and dread.

He could have her forever. Maybe it would be all right.

"You look terrible." Chrissy peered at him. "Let me make you coffee and something to eat. You can tell us all about it."

****

Three hours later, showered, clad in clean clothes, and with his headache died down to a dull throb, Brendan presented himself at Mary Grace's place of work. He'd debated as to whether he should stop by a jeweler's on the way and buy a ring. What was a marriage proposal without a ring, after all? Thing was, he couldn't be completely sure he had proposed—or

147

that he hadn't. It made his stomach queasy.

He found Mary Grace in the business office, looking harried and frazzled. Was a newly engaged woman supposed to look like that?

Darcy, also there, looked up with a big smile and rose to her feet. "There now, Grace, you can get it all straightened out. I'll give you some privacy."

She left the office and shut the door behind her. Brendan stood gazing at Mary Grace; she returned his look with exasperation.

"What am I to do with you, Brendan O'Rourke? It's all over town that you asked me to marry you."

"I know, I'm sorry. I didn't say a word, honestly."

"No, it was Mrs. Senet from across the hall. She must have been down the shops as soon as they opened and told what she saw. She's a terrible gossip."

"It doesn't matter. Mary Grace—"

"Of course it matters. There's my reputation—and yours. It seems the whole town thinks we're engaged."

"Thinks?" Brendan drew a breath that hurt. "We're not, then?"

She stared at him. "You mean you don't remember?"

"I was awfully drunk, Mary Grace. I swear to God, I'll never drink again."

She snorted her derision. "As if I believe that!"

"No more whiskey, then."

She charged up to him, glaring. "You thought we were engaged? You came here thinking—thinking you asked me to marry you? That I said 'yes'?"

Brendan flinched. "Easy, Mary Grace. My head's about to come off."

"And what kind of marriage proposal would that

be, if you couldn't even remember it?"

"Pretty poor."

"One spurred by liquor!"

"I know it's not ideal. But I supposed you might have taken pity on me. Charlie said—"

"Oh, will you forget about Charlie? There's no ghost in that house. Stop blaming your actions on someone else."

"I'm not. And don't be angry with me, Mary Grace."

"How do you expect me to feel? Now we have to set the whole city of St. John's straight."

"We're definitely not engaged then?"

"We are not."

Brendan choked back his disappointment. "I'll take care of it, Mary Grace."

"How?" she challenged.

Good question. "I'll make an announcement the next time we play. Or maybe," he added wryly, "I should just stop by Mrs. Senet's."

"Well, that's not humiliating, is it? Not a bit!" she flared.

"Would you rather I just asked you to marry me? Here and now? Make it true?"

They stared at each other for the span of twenty heartbeats while the color drained from Mary Grace's face.

"Would you?"

Brendan thought about it. "Yes."

"But that's no reason to get engaged, is it? Just because St. John's thinks we are."

How about because I can't live without you? Because I want you so much I can barely breathe? But he couldn't say those things in the face of her obvious distress.

The prospect of marrying him put that look in her eyes. God damn it. He might just as well go off and jump in the ocean.

Chapter Twenty-One

"Brendan O'Rourke. Hsst! Brendan O'Rourke, come in here."

The appeal issued from the doorway of Kregler's Jewelers as Brendan passed by on his way back home. Tommy Kregler stood there gesturing to him urgently.

Brendan had known Tommy—a friend of his father's—all his life. Now he stepped into the shop to find it empty of everyone but Tommy himself, who beamed at him.

"I understand congratulations are in order. She's a lovely girl, just lovely! I always thought back when you were dating, before you went away, you were perfect for each other. And she waited for you all these years, didn't she? Left poor Chet Hader at the altar. Must be true love."

"Uh—" Brendan managed to cough out half a word. "It might not be quite like that."

"You'll be needing a ring. Something worthy of your love. You've come to the right place."

"I didn't actually come—"

"You know I sold Chet the ring he presented her. And it was a nice ring, a very nice ring. You'll have to go one better, won't you? Don't worry, I have just the thing. From my private stock. I assume money is no object?"

"Well, I don't think—"

"No, that's not the kind of thing a man scrimps over, is it? And it's not as if you need to worry about money, is it? Rich as Croesus, I understand."

"I wouldn't say—"

Tommy beamed at him. "Come through to the back room. You'll want to wow her, make her glad she said 'yes.' "

"Can a ring do that?"

"Oh, Lord, yes. The setting now, the setting must be perfect. And the stone must represent your love."

"I don't think that's possible."

"You'd be surprised. I heard through the grapevine you hadn't presented her with a ring as yet. I was sure you'd have the good sense to come to me."

In the back room, spread on a table under a spotlight, were several velvet-lined cases, each holding about a dozen rings. Brendan stared at them in fascination. He wasn't buying a ring. Of course not. But if he were…

"Now, Grace Dawe," Tommy mused. "What color setting, do you think? There's gold, platinum, titanium…"

"Gold. Definitely."

"What color?"

"Gold's yellow, isn't it?"

"Goodness, no, not all of it. There's white gold, red gold—"

"Red gold? There really is such a thing?"

"Oh, yes. It's a bit richer in hue." Tommy gave him a speculative look. "I have some rings here from Ireland."

Brendan's eyebrows flew up. "Ireland, eh?"

"I import from a jeweler in Dublin. Only look at

these."

Brendan looked where indicated and blew a whistle between his teeth. Diamonds large and small sat on intricately-worked bands. Even to his untutored eye the craftsmanship looked exquisite.

"Beautiful."

"That's the idea—as beautiful as your love."

Brendan grunted. He doubted Bridget O'Rourke ever had anything but a plain band. Maybe it was time he did something different from Charlie. Following in his footsteps sure as hell wasn't working.

He scanned the rows of rings carefully, his eye always coming back to one. It had a rich, dark gold setting and a band all chased with Celtic knotwork around a square-cut diamond.

"Is that red gold?"

"Irish gold, yes. You have an excellent eye. That's an exquisite ring."

How would it look on Mary Grace's hand? Like it belonged there, like she belonged to him at last. For all time.

He swallowed and went a bit dizzy for a minute.

"How much is it?"

"Now, Brendan, you can't put a price tag on love."

"It's free, then?"

Tommy chuckled. "Hardly. But I could let you take it on approval, seeing as I know you so well. See if Mary Grace likes it. If she doesn't, you can bring it back. Bring her in and let her choose."

"How could she fail to like that?"

"How, indeed? The designer put a magic charm inside. Look." Tommy snatched the ring up and showed it to Brendan. "It's inscribed in the Gaelic. Bestows love unending."

"Does it, now?"

"You think she'd like that?"

Brendan couldn't force words past the lump in his throat.

"Look, let me box it up for you. You take it with you and give it to her tonight."

"It might take a day or two—"

"Fine, fine. You just take your time pleasing your lady, Brendan O'Rourke."

If only he could.

****

"Now, that's a pretty bauble. Enough to tickle any woman's fancy. You've done well, son, very well."

The ring sat in its open box on the kitchen table where both Brendan and Charlie could eye it. "You think so?"

"I do. Get her over here and present it to her tonight."

"Why here? Why not at her apartment?"

"So's I can watch, of course."

Brendan grunted, not at all sure he'd done the right thing. On the way home from Kregler's, with the ring in his pocket, he'd met no less than three people who'd congratulated him on his engagement. He'd failed to correct any of them, even though Mary Grace had left the matter in his hands.

It seemed all his hope had not died. If he asked her properly and she accepted, they'd need to make no corrections.

Knocking sounded at the front door. Charlie winked out of sight, and Brendan hurried to open the door, where he found two constables.

"Mr. O'Rourke?" asked the female officer. "Do you recognize this?"

She held up his fiddle case.

"Isolde! You found her?"

"If you mean the instrument, yes, we did, only this morning. The thief placed an online ad and was attempting to sell the remains of Brendan O'Rourke's fiddle for a thousand dollars."

Brendan's heart fell. "The remains?"

"May we come in?"

"Yes, sure."

Once in the parlor, the constable opened Isolde's case and revealed the fiddle inside. Isolde lay in two pieces, connected only by her strings.

Brendan swore with feeling. "She smashed it?"

"Seems she was very angry. Claims you played a cruel practical joke on her. Is that true?"

"No. And even if I had, that's no excuse to destroy a valuable and treasured instrument."

"Sorry, sir," said the second constable. "It was in this condition when we recovered it. Do you think it can be repaired?"

Brendan picked Isolde up carefully. "I don't know." Good thing Bridget had saved Charlie's instrument. At least he still had that.

"We'll need you to come down to the station to press charges."

"Is the thief in lockup now?"

"She is. Do you want to see her?"

Brendan shuddered. "No. I'll stop in later this afternoon."

The constables turned to leave. The female smiled at him. "Oh, and Mr. O'Rourke, congratulations on your engagement."

****

Grace steamed her way through the afternoon, turning away congratulations and inquiries as to the date of her wedding while wishing Brendan O'Rourke would get off the stick and correct the misconceptions besetting the city. Just how he was supposed to do that, she couldn't say. But the rumor seemed to be spreading rather than dying down.

Ready to leave the museum at six o'clock, she walked out only to find Brendan standing next to her car. Her heart leaped and then sank in a sickening seesaw of dread and desire.

The last thing she needed.

"How are you feeling, Brendan?"

"I'm fine, Mary Grace. We need to talk. Come back to the house with me."

"So we can have a threesome—you, me, and the ghost?"

"So I can ask you an important question."

"I don't think so."

"Come for dinner, then. Give me a chance here, Mary Grace. I'm trying."

She gave him a closer look and saw the tension that scored his face, the misery in his eyes. Rarely could she remember Brendan O'Rourke looking miserable. Those eyes usually brimmed with happy confidence, sparkled with life and humor. Or smoldered with desire.

"I hope you've been busy informing people this engagement debacle is a mistake."

"Debacle, is it?"

"Yes. Obviously."

"Not so simple, Mary Grace. The news has spread

like wildfire. Am I supposed to go door to door? Take out an ad in the paper?"

"I don't know."

"That's what we have to talk about."

Grace sighed. "All right, but I don't want to argue with you anymore. I'm too tired. Some maniac kept me up half the night."

"Welcome to my world," he muttered.

"How did you get here? I don't see your parents' car."

"Well, I set out walking."

"Walking! Are you mad?"

"But no fewer than four people offered me rides along the way. The woman who dropped me off is a friend of Mrs. Taylor's."

"Get in the car. I'll drive."

Brendan complied, looking a tad more cheerful. Inside the car, Grace caught his scent—a hint of the soap he always favored and the irresistible smell of Brendan. Maybe this wasn't such a good idea.

"If you're interested," he said as she pulled out of the car park, "Mrs. Taylor's friend says Mrs. Taylor's niece, Jenny, has been spending every night with Barry Tate. Apparently it's quite the scandal."

"God help the girl."

"No, this is a good thing. Remember, Mrs. Taylor tried to fix Jenny up with me. Anyway, Jenny's the one who made the aphrodisiac-laden trifle."

Mary Grace shot him a look. "There isn't any of that at your house, is there?"

"There is not."

"Or any of that burnt pasta sauce from the other night?"

"No."

"Or Johnny and his girlfriend?"

"They've gone to the hotel."

"The ghost?"

Brendan shifted uncomfortably in his seat. "He's still there. I need to find a way to get rid of him. Any ideas?"

"Seriously? You're asking me for ways to banish your great-grandfather?"

"I am. He's a terrible pest."

"Why didn't the exorcism work?"

"Apparently it was a blessing and not a proper exorcism. And it had no effect on him because he'd already been excommunicated."

"I see. You can't just chase him out?"

"He appears to be rooted to the house—can't go anywhere else, really."

"Why?"

"Eh?"

Grace repeated patiently, "Why's he rooted to the house? What does he need?"

Brendan gave her an uneasy look. "To reform me. To keep me from making the same mistakes he did where my love life is concerned."

Grace gave a hard laugh. "Not doing a great job of it, is he?"

"I can't say he is. Most the advice he's given me so far has been bad. I'm hoping to change that tonight."

"Just—no funny stuff."

"Funny stuff?"

"Yes. Remember, Brendan, I'm not staying the night."

Chapter Twenty-Two

"Did I tell you the constables recovered Isolde?"

Brendan, not sure he wanted to reintroduce the subject of him having brought home another woman, nevertheless felt desperate for a topic of conversation. So far the evening had not gone well. It was one thing to create pretty little scenarios in his head wherein Mary Grace took one look at the ring—still in his pocket at this juncture—and tumbled into his arms. But making them come true would require a bit of orchestration.

Mary Grace seemed tense and edgy, had barely touched the meal he'd prepared, and kept looking around as if expecting to see Charlie pop into sight. So far Charlie hadn't showed, not so much as a wisp of him.

Now she looked interested. "That's grand news, Brendan."

"It is, and it isn't. She's damaged. Let me show you." He fixed her with a stare. "She's up in my room, if you would care…"

"I would not."

"I'll fetch her down, then."

He bounded up the stairs to his room. On the way back down he wondered how he was going to manage maneuvering into position on his knees so he could present the ring.

"Kiss her," Charlie whispered in his ear.

"You keep quiet. And stay out of sight."

Mary Grace exclaimed in dismay over Isolde, touched her broken spine with what looked like genuine grief, and smoothed her strings.

"Oh, Brendan, how awful. I know what she meant to you. Can she be mended?"

"I doubt it."

"It's like a death in the family."

"It is, yes."

He'd taken the opportunity to sit down next to her on the chesterfield, as close as he dared. He reached his arm around her in order to stroke Isolde's shredded wood and Mary Grace leaned into him just a bit.

Damn if Charlie didn't have the right idea. At last.

The kiss lasted so long Brendan forgot about breathing. He didn't care. The taste of her went straight to his head; the warmth of her in his arms had his heart pounding. She eased up against him, relaxing for the first time all night.

Was this all she'd been wanting? A kiss?

He'd better make it a good one then. No trouble there. He caressed the inside of her mouth with his tongue, falling into a natural rhythm that mimicked what they'd shared before. She melted further, gave a funny little moan, and wound her arms around his neck. Her breasts contacted his chest, and he caught fire.

When the kiss ended—perhaps an hour or so later—they both struggled to catch their breath.

Would this be a good time to slide down to his knees? To pull out the box in his pocket? To ask her upstairs?

Should he present the ring to her in bed?

"Brendan." She groaned his name before withdrawing her arms from around his neck, only to shove her hands up under his shirt where they stroked their way through the hair on his chest. "I shouldn't be here. This is the last thing I should be doing."

"Don't say that, darlin'."

"But everything's such a mess. With the rumors, and the band—"

"For God's sake, don't bring up the band."

"I absolutely should not go upstairs with you to that room where we first made love. But I want to. I do." She almost wept the last two words.

Brendan made no reply but put his fingers into action. She still wore the costume from the museum, and he went to work on the bodice.

When he was halfway there, she began helping him. The bodice opened and she fell into his hands.

"My God, Mary Grace, you're beautiful."

"You think so?"

"I know so."

"But"—she punctuated the words with little kisses as he stroked her with his thumbs—"I'm sure you've seen…much more…exciting women."

"Impossible. There's no one more exciting than you."

"Good answer."

"You want proof?" He directed her hand to his lap, where he now wore a bulge of iron. "Mary Grace, I don't want to assume anything. I've made that mistake before."

"Assume?" She began massaging him through his jeans.

"Are we going to make love?"

161

Not satisfied with her ministrations, she unfastened his pants and shoved her hands inside. "It looks that way."

"Here or upstairs?"

Hands still caressing him intimately, she looked into his eyes. For an instant they had another of those moments when time stopped. All he could see was Mary Grace's eyes, and her soul simmering there.

"Upstairs. But I hope I'm not going to regret this. I don't need any more regret."

"I won't let you regret it, darlin'."

He caught her up in his arms and climbed the stairs.

****

Grace, moving with heavy-limbed languor, stirred in the bed and pried open eyes weighted by satisfaction. The room had undergone a transformation since she'd last been here—Brendan's mom must have redecorated. But her feelings remained pretty much the same—warm and sated, teetering on the edge of wanting more.

She always wanted more from this man. Maybe that was part of the problem.

Oh, what had she gone and done? Exactly what she'd promised herself she wouldn't. Again.

Why couldn't she resist Brendan O'Rourke?

At least this time he'd used a condom. Cherry flavored. She wondered idly what other flavors he kept in the drawer.

She shouldn't stay to find out. She should get up now, put on her clothes, and walk out of here while she still could.

Instead she turned her head and looked at Brendan in the dim light coming through the front window. Her heart did a funny, painful flip.

He sprawled beside her like the answer to a maiden's dream—her dream, anyway, though she certainly could no longer claim maidenhood. That ship had sailed years ago—with him. She'd had other men since—one or two. None touched what she felt for him.

She loved the way he tasted, the way he felt beneath her fingers. Loved the way he smiled, especially when he gave her that slow grin during sex. She loved...

Him?

No, no, no. She'd meant what she said the other night at her place when he went down on his knees. She had to protect herself at all costs. Because she wouldn't survive losing him again.

"Brendan," she whispered, "I should go."

"Not yet." One long arm snaked out and drew her against his side. He trailed a calloused finger down her cheek. "Stay."

She went weak from her lips to her heels. Would a few hours make a difference? One night?

It might. "I can't stay."

His eyes opened; he regarded her with a possessive hazel stare that warmed her blood.

Oh, not again—she really wasn't going to make love to him again, not at a single look. Was she?

"Damn you, Brendan O'Rourke."

"What? Why?"

"A thousand reasons. For being so good-looking. For knowing just how to touch me so I—" She broke off.

He gave her the lazy smile, the one that affected her so profoundly. "I didn't hear you complaining a few minutes ago." Devilry danced in his eyes. "Perhaps it's because your mouth was otherwise occupied, eh?"

Perhaps. Damn him.

She let her gaze trail down his body slowly. Perfection. But she suspected if he had stumpy legs and three eyes she'd still want him.

He moved his fingers from her cheek to her breast, a coaxing motion. "Don't leave yet. I have to ask you something."

"What is it?"

A new look invaded his eyes. Was that uncertainty?

"Kiss me."

Request or demand? Grace had no chance to decide. He claimed her mouth with hunger that should have been answered by their previous activities but obviously wasn't.

Oh, God, oh, God, she *was* going to make love to him again.

But she fought her way free from the spell his lips wove and planted her hands against his chest. "What do you have to ask me?"

"First things first. Touch me."

She already was, her fingers stroking without her permission. Warmth flooded through her along with a feeling she hadn't known in eight years, that she was where she needed to be, that she wanted this and nothing else.

He cupped her face between his hands and kissed her again before he said, "You're so lovely, every inch of you right down to that freckle on your—" He slid his hands down all the way to her butt and drew her against him so pertinent areas meshed.

Grace gasped.

"When I'm with you, Mary Grace, it's like time stands still. Like it ceases to exist. Like we're the same people we were."

"But we're not." She thought she'd better throw that in there, even though she really didn't want to interrupt the fantasy he created.

"We are," he insisted, "in all the ways that count. In the forever parts."

Her eyes opened wide at the beauty of his words.

"I—" she began, but he stopped her words with a third kiss. Three makes the charm, she thought as the spell became complete. No longer able to think, she could only feel.

Hours later a sound penetrated her sleep—that of the dead, or the utterly satisfied. It teased her ear with soft persistence, a beautiful undulation that came and went like music on the wind.

It *was* music—fiddle music—a slow, beguiling tune plaintive enough to pierce the heart. She lay still, barely breathing, and wondered whether she dreamed.

For the room lay in darkness; morning had not yet come. Brendan, she decided. He must have risen and taken out the fiddle to play. And if that was so...

Emotion flooded her heart to breaking, making it hard to breathe. Brendan's music always reflected his feelings. And this, if ever she'd heard one, sounded like a love song.

How could she doubt him, then?

Tears filled her eyes, and she blinked them away fiercely, straining to see. There—a tall, thin outline by the window, only dimly seen, the music flowing from his fingers like love from his heart.

It took her a dozen breaths to realize Brendan still lay beside her, warm and fast asleep beneath her hands.

Chapter Twenty-Three

"I tell you Brendan, I saw him. And heard him, too."

"I believe you, darling." Brendan pulled Mary Grace into his arms and up against his body. She'd awakened him at four in the morning, babbling with excitement and wonder, and had barely stopped talking since. Now, the day had strengthened and full sunlight poured through the kitchen windows, and showed him the emotions teeming in her eyes.

Beautiful, blue-gray eyes. Beautiful woman, keeper of his heart. By God, what was wrong with him? He wanted her again.

But she'd already fitted herself into her costume and pinned up her hair—an alluring process that almost took him back to his knees. And she just kept talking.

"Such wonderful music, Brendan. You never said he played so well."

"Did I not tell you he was here? Mary Grace, did you think I was making up stories?"

"I'm not sure what I thought. It's different actually seeing and hearing him." She reflected on it. "His playing sounds an awful lot like yours. And oh, such a song! Full of longing."

"He's longing for his Bridget." Brendan bent his head and kissed Mary Grace on lips already swollen from his attentions last night.

She drew away from him. "Tell me again, why is he separated from her? If they're both dead, can't they just go"—she waved her hand—"wherever people's souls go?"

"You'd think so, wouldn't you? But Charlie says Bridget hasn't forgiven him for his manifold sins."

Mary Grace gazed at Brendan seriously. "If she truly loved him, she'd forgive him anything."

For an instant Brendan's heart stood still. "Is that so?"

"It is." She leaned up and kissed him softly.

"Well, the thing is, I don't think Charlie believes that. He told me Bridget's gone on without him to wherever good souls go. And he can't reach her."

"He's rooted here, you said."

"Haunting the place, playing music—drunk all the time. I believe he's convinced if he can salvage my life and keep me from making the same mistakes he did he can somehow redeem himself."

"What mistakes?"

"Not paying Bridget the attention she deserved, neglecting his duty to her. Choosing music over his wife and child."

"I see. And"—she swallowed visibly—"do you intend to follow his advice?"

"Is there a chance I can redeem myself in your eyes, Mary Grace?"

"If Charlie can, you can. And I believe we need to do everything we can to help Charlie on his way. He's suffered enough, don't you think?"

"I do. But how can we help?"

"I can't keep from believing if Bridget heard what I heard last night—well, his heart was in that music he played."

"Was it?"

"Oh, yes, and it was so beautiful. If that's a reflection of how he loves Bridget, what can she do but forgive him?"

"And, Mary Grace, if a man's music is the only way he can truly express what's in his heart?"

She gazed at him for a long moment. "Then a woman better learn to stop being annoyed with him and listen." She tipped her head. "Which reminds me—what did you want to ask me last night?"

"It can wait now. You need to get to work."

"I'm already late. Good thing I'm the director. I don't suppose I'll find it necessary to fire myself."

He laid his hands on her shoulders. "Mary Grace, come back here after you finish work. Spend another night with me."

She considered it, and he feared she would shake her head. "I'll give it some thought."

Well, at least she hadn't said no.

She went out and climbed into her car. The next door over opened, and Gord Kennedy stuck his head out.

"Congratulations on your engagement, Brendan. I suppose that was you and Grace celebrating last night?"

They hadn't been that loud, had they? He remembered only murmurs, mostly of satisfaction.

"It was, yes. Sorry if we disturbed you."

"Not at all, old son. Keep it up. That sweet song put my missus in the mood, if you know what I mean." Gord wagged his eyebrows.

"Uh—glad to hear it. Any time I can further the cause of true love."

Gord watched Mary Grace's car pull away. "Is Grace living here with you now?"

"I hope so, Gord. I can only hope so."

Back in the kitchen, Brendan found Charlie waiting for him, floating in the vicinity of the table.

"So, lad, perhaps you'll explain yourself."

Brendan raised his eyebrows. "I beg your pardon?"

"All that kissing and hugging and hanky-panky last night, yet you never asked her the question—nor gave her the ring. And here's me thinking you intended to mend your ways."

Brendan scowled at his great-grandfather. "I hope you weren't watching."

"Of course not." Charlie laid a ghostly hand on his chest. "Would I do anything so indecent? I would not have wanted anyone spying on me when my Bridget and I got…well, romantically inclined."

"Then how do you know what I did or didn't say?"

"I've ears, haven't I? At least spectral ones, so to speak. Anyway, I just popped in once or twice to see how you progressed."

"You call that decent?"

"All I can say is the girl must truly love you. For any young lady to grant such favors without benefit of a wedding ring…"

Brendan shuffled in embarrassment. "Things are a lot different now than they were in your day."

"Apparently so." Charlie leaned toward him. "Back then, even most prostitutes wouldn't do those things, and if they did you had to pay them extra."

"Yes, well."

"Must be the benefit of choosing a non-Catholic girl, eh?"

"I'm not sure that has much to do with it."

"You'd be surprised. Anyway, when I think of it, with all that activity I suppose it's understandable you didn't get 'round to giving her the ring."

"I want it to be special when I give it to her—a real moment."

"Ah, I understand. I officially asked my Bridget to marry me by moonlight."

"Did you, now?"

"I'd just finished playing a set and had taken a wee bit too much to drink."

"Imagine that."

"Trouble is, I'd promised to come by the house that night—she'd made me supper, and we were going to spend a few hours together, just sitting and talking. That was before I stopped in for a drink on the way and met some fellows. Long story short, by the time I got here she was pretty angry."

"I'll bet."

"My Bridget angry was a sight to be seen. Not a screamer, nor a yeller, lad, and she never threw things at me. Instead she'd go all cold and quiet, which was ten times harder to bear. She'd haul up her indignation and freeze me with it.

"I remember fine what she said to me that night, just before she stopped talking altogether. 'You needn't think you can treat me like an afterthought, Charles Michael O'Rourke.' "

Brendan snorted.

A stricken look came over the ghost's face. "Yes, shameful, isn't it? The poor lass would have been better off walking away from me then." Charlie eyed his great-grandson. "Of course then you would not exist."

"Thank you, Grandmother Bridget. So how did the proposal come about?"

"Well, I was full of remorse and aching to put things right between us. Believe it as you may, I couldn't stand it when Bridget was upset with me. I still can't. 'Tis torture for a man, lad, when he upsets his woman."

"Yet you did, again and again."

"Yes." Charlie sighed. "Just like you."

"Get to the proposal."

"I told her what she needed was a walk in the moonlight. I knew just what a lovely night it was, see, with a full moon. We walked down toward the harbor, and it was magical, just magical. I sang her a song—"

"You can sing?"

"To be sure. Anyway, I'd left Guinevere behind, and the moment called for music. Bridget looked so beautiful with the dusty moonlight in her eyes and shining on the oval of her face...did I tell you she had an oval face? Just perfect. And that bonny, bonny hair of red-gold..."

He's still in love with her, so much in love, Brendan thought, and swallowed a sudden lump in his throat. The poor cuss.

More gently he asked, "What song did you sing?"

" 'Bridget O'Malley.' Do you know it?"

Brendan nodded. "Beautiful."

"And there in the moonlight I was overcome. I told her I could not live without her. I told her she possessed my heart. I begged her to marry me and said if she did I would change my ways, become a refined man and disappoint her no more."

"She believed you."

"She did, bless her, and gave me a kiss, one of the sweetest kisses ever bestowed, right there in the moonlight overlooking the harbor. But," Charlie continued wretchedly, "I did not keep my promise. I disappointed her time after time and then left her alone. How could she do anything but go ahead without me, now, eh?"

Brendan, filled with sympathy for Charlie, said nothing. He'd been close enough to where Charlie stood, often enough, to feel his pain.

And yes, there was a lesson to be learned here: He'd better not make promises he didn't mean to keep.

Chapter Twenty-Four

"What's this I hear? You're engaged to Brendan O'Rourke?"

Grace spun from the display in Andrews' Drug Store to find Chet Hader standing behind her, glowering. She eyed him in dismay. Though she'd dated Chet for nearly two years, she had rarely seen him angry. But he looked flaming hot now.

Embarrassment stained her cheeks. She'd finished up at work and decided to swing by Andrews' for a few essentials before driving to Brendan's. How inauspicious that she should encounter Chet now.

Her discomfort made her defensive. "What's it to you, Chet?"

"What's it to me? Four months ago I expected you to be my wife. That's what."

Grace glanced around. Other shoppers were already staring. "I don't want to talk about it, especially here."

"Then we'll go outside."

"I don't think…"

"At the moment, Grace, I don't care what you think. Don't you suppose you owe me ten minutes?"

Grace nodded and put down her intended purchases to follow Chet from the store, which had gone uncannily quiet.

Out on the street she glanced around; this didn't

seem much better. "Come to my car," she told him.

He followed her to the spot where she'd parked but then stood with his hand on the roof of the vehicle.

"Just tell me, Grace. Is it true or not?"

"Not. At least…"

He broke in on her. "So why's it all over town?"

"A misunderstanding turned into a rumor. But—"

"Then why are you in Andrews' buying… You're sleeping with the guy, aren't you? My God, you actually went back to him."

"Chet—"

"I can't believe you went back to him. And I can't believe I thought when all the craziness died down you'd actually come back to me."

"Chet, I told you when we talked at the museum that will never happen."

"Yeah, well, you also told me over and over, when we were together, you'd never go back to that—arse, I think you called him. Yeah, that's it, a selfish, arrogant arse who'd two-timed you with his music once too often. The whole time we were seeing each other you never shut up about it."

"Well, pardon me if I was a bore."

Chet ignored that. "But now he crooks his finger and you go running back like a little puppy. So forgive me if I don't believe a word you say."

"I guess maybe you had a lucky escape, eh?"

"I guess maybe I did. Have a happy life, Grace, following him around and waiting for him to toss you whatever crumbs of his attention he can spare. I would have put you first. So who's the stupid arse?"

"Me. I'm the stupid arse, Chet."

Still spitting mad, he glared at her. "Just tell me

one thing—is he the reason you left me at the altar? The real reason?"

Grace bowed her head as grief, acknowledgement, and regret flooded her in equal measures. "Yes. The truth is, Chet, I can't imagine myself with him. But I can't imagine myself with anyone else. I hope someday you'll find it in your heart to forgive me."

"Just like you've forgiven Brendan O'Rourke? Don't count on it, Grace."

He slapped the hood of her car, spun, and made his way off up the street, leaving Grace aching.

****

"Let us in, b'y. We've some news."

Brendan balked when he found all three of his fellow band members—plus Chrissy—on his doorstep, carrying their instruments.

Johnny, in the lead, barked at him, "We've rehearsing to do and decisions to make."

Brendan hesitated before moving aside. He'd been expecting Mary Grace for the last half hour, overanxious and hungry for her. The last thing he wanted to see was this crew at his door. "What's the news? 'Cause this isn't a good time."

They ignored him and filed past into the parlor, where they began to set up.

"You want to rehearse? Here? Now?"

Rory Sullivan gave him a droll smile. "Looks that way, don't it?"

"But I'm expecting someone." He cleared his throat. "For the night."

That made Johnny bend a look on him. "If you're talking about Grace, she'll just have to get used to it again, like Chrissy here. Right, Chris? Maybe you can make friends with the girl, give each other some company while we're occupied."

"That would be nice." Chrissy beamed. "We can make coffee for you guys. And sandwiches."

"Hell with that," said Ned, breaking out his accordion. "You can keep our glasses full."

"We've a lot to celebrate," Johnny said. "I just had a call from Brett Muskowitz. He wants to know if it's true Kissin' the Cod's back together for good."

Brett Muskowitz was their agent. "He heard about us all the way back in Chicago?"

"We're big news, b'y." Johnny looked Brendan straight in the eye. "I told him it's true. Now you tell us I didn't lie."

Confounded, Brendan stared at his fellow band members. At that moment, a knock sounded at the door.

He hurried out, knowing in his heart who he'd see standing there. Perfect timing, and what the hell was he going to say to her?

He didn't expect her to be upset, flushed with what looked like anger, distress brimming in her eyes.

"Sorry I'm late. I had a run-in at Andrews'."

"That's all right. Mary Grace…"

"In fact, we need to talk. About where this thing's going between us."

Brendan seized her arms. "We will, darlin'. But—"

"About your intentions. My intentions. And whether we're just making the same mistakes over again. It can't just be about the sex."

From the parlor issued a note squeezed out of Rory's accordion, followed by a chord from Johnny's guitar. The color drained from Mary Grace's face, leaving her pale as Charlie O'Rourke.

She freed herself from Brendan's grip, moved past him and into the parlor, where she froze, staring like a woman in a dream.

"What's all this?"

"We're rehearsing," Johnny called cheerfully. "It's what I was just about to tell our Brendan—Kissin' the Cod's back in business. We've a big date scheduled here in St. John's this weekend and a huge tour on tap. Our agent just set it up."

"Tour?" Brendan and Mary Grace repeated in unison.

All three band members—plus Chrissy—beamed. "Europe," Johnny chortled. "Can you believe it, b'y?"

****

"I didn't know, Mary Grace. I swear I didn't. It was as much a surprise to me as to you. Johnny's always been the main contact with Muskowitz. He has the better head for business, see. Maybe that was a mistake on my part…"

He stopped talking and looked at her. It had taken him half an hour to chase everyone from his house. In the end, he'd only accomplished it with promises they'd meet again tomorrow.

"No time to waste," Johnny had said in a dire tone when he and Chrissy left. "Europe, Brendan—our big break."

He'd half expected Mary Grace to leave also. To his surprise she'd stayed, but he sensed something very wrong. Now she sat perched on his mother's chesterfield, with her elbows on her knees and her face in her hands. She hadn't said a word, and that made Brendan nervous.

Very, very nervous.

"Mary Grace, darlin'?" He sat beside her and to his horror saw she wept into her hands silently. "No, oh, no—don't do that. I can't stand it."

He pulled her into his arms, fast against his chest. Mary Grace seldom wept. She raged, she flamed—upon occasion she swore. Tears worried him.

"What did you come here to tell me, my love?"

She mopped her cheeks and pulled away just far enough to look into his eyes. "That it's me."

"What? I don't follow."

"I ran into Chet at Andrews'. He made me see it wasn't all your fault we broke up. It was me too—maybe even mostly me. I'm not a very nice person, Brendan. I treated him as shabbily as you treated me."

"Wait a minute, wait a minute." Brendan fished for the vital point. "Have we broke up—again?"

"Well, of course. So I came here ready to—to—" She waved her hands. "And I find it all happening again. Nothing's changed. Nothing will ever change."

"You can't say that. Listen to me; I had every intention of devoting this evening to you. The fellas just showed up. And Europe—it's…"

"Your big break." She gave a brittle laugh. "Where have I heard that before? Just like playing Fitzgerald's was your big break. Playing Halifax. Boston. Philly. Chicago. Going into the studio was your big break. What made me think—?"

"This."

He kissed her, a kiss with all his passion behind it. He poured himself into her the way he usually poured himself into his music, with a totality that left room for nothing else. As soon as she began to respond he gathered her in and carried her up the steep narrow stairs to his bed, for once sparing nary a thought for Charlie O'Rourke. No one—and nothing—existed for him but Mary Grace Dawe.

He undressed her slowly in the dark, quiet room, and they both trembled with need. This time when he came to her it had little to do with gratification and everything to do with devotion.

"I love you," he told her when they lay joined and complete. "I always have. I never, never stopped. Not"—kiss—"for"—kiss—"one"—kiss—"moment."

She began to weep again, silent tears trickling down onto his pillow. "Oh, God, Brendan. Oh, God."

"Don't be upset, my beautiful, beautiful girl. Just tell me you love me."

"I do. You know I do. That was never the problem."

"I don't want to hear about problems, Mary Grace. This is too perfect." He flexed himself, still inside her. "Can't you feel how perfect it is?"

She wept harder. He kissed the tears away. "Listen to me. Listen to me, Mary Grace. Is this about the music? If it's still about the music, I'll give it up. Here and now, hear me? I'll tell the boys to find another fiddle player and go off to Europe."

"You can't do that."

"I can. Fiddle players are a dime a dozen."

"Not like you."

"They'll find someone."

She stared into his face, her eyes wide and awash with tears. "And what would you do then, Brendan O'Rourke? What, with the better part of you given away?"

He shrugged. "I'll get a job here in St. John's. To

tell you the truth, I have a nice little nest egg built up. I never did spend money on much but ale. We'll be all right, Mary Grace."

"Oh, Brendan—oh, Brendan. I might be all right. You? Never!"

"You just let me worry about that. This is what you've always wanted, isn't it? For me to see the truth, that you're more important to me than anything. Well, I've seen it at last. I'm there, darlin'. You and Charlie helped me see my way."

She said nothing. He trailed his lips across her cheek to her ear.

"Why are you still crying? Why aren't you smothering me with kisses of joy?"

"Because." She moved suddenly, pulled from him and turned away. "What does that make me, if I ask you to give up the band?"

"You're not asking me to give up anything. That's what I'm telling you here. I'll freely sacrifice—"

"A relationship can't survive on sacrifice. Chet taught me that. Charlie and Bridget should have made it clear." Mary Grace gulped. "That's what I came here to tell you, Brendan. I've blamed you all this time for everything that went wrong between us. But I was just as much wrong—just as selfish—as you were. I knew who you were when I fell in love with you. A musician to the bone."

"Well then." Brendan's mind scrambled. "That's good. Surely this is good; we can come to some sort of understanding."

"Can we?"

"Yes."

"But I still don't know if I can live with sharing

you, selfish witch that I am. But I can't live with giving you up, either. What's to do?"

A good question. All this while, Brendan had been sure Mary Grace wanted only to reform him. Now it seemed she wanted to reform herself also.

Chapter Twenty-Five

Lying there in the dark, Grace could feel Brendan's bewilderment. She couldn't blame him for feeling bewildered—at the moment she barely understood her own feelings.

And he, poor man, had just given her the greatest gift of which he could conceive, one he thought she'd always wanted.

And she had, she had. She'd spent all the worst moments of their relationship wishing he'd put her— put their love—first. Now he did.

And it felt terrible.

Better ask him to cut off a foot to be with her. To sever a hand or dig his own heart from his chest.

So here they lay together, naked and warm, and all she could do was grieve.

"I should go," she decided. "We need some space." She moved in the bed and slid away from him, though it was the last thing she wanted to do.

"We've had our space, Mary Grace. Eight years."

But she had to get away from him right now, get away from these feelings. *Fool. You'll just take them with you.*

That realization stopped her cold in mid-hunt for her clothes, most of which had ended up on the floor. She might have run eight years ago, gone bouncing around the world in an effort to outdistance her pain.

She'd been a girl then, but she was a woman now and couldn't run from this.

Perched on the edge of the bed, she turned and looked at him. He appeared little more than a shadow, long and lean, pricked out in dim light from outside. She couldn't see what lay in his eyes, but she ached for wanting him.

"You're so beautiful, Mary Grace. Don't put those clothes on."

"Sex won't solve anything."

"Won't it? Then tell me why I only feel whole when you're in my arms."

"Habit? Hormones?"

"Habit. Don't you think that would have been broken during the last eight years? Yet all I had to do was see you again. Listen to me, Mary Grace." He caught her hand. "I don't want to make the mistakes Charlie made."

"Poor Charlie."

"I know—can you imagine? Grieving for the woman he loves for eternity. I don't want to do that; I don't want to be that."

"But your music, Brendan. I don't want you grieving for that, either."

"I've had that, had the fame and the fortune. It's time for a new part of my life to begin."

"You don't mean that."

"Shall I prove it to you?" He moved suddenly. "Then I will. Go ahead, get dressed, Mary Grace. We're going out."

"Out? Now? It must be the middle of the night."

"That's the best time. And give me your car keys. I'm driving."

****

The streets lay nearly silent. The city of St. John's slept bathed in the light of a full moon, all black and silver, with the sea, quiet as a pool, lying beyond.

Brendan parked the car in the lot—now empty—beside George's Pond on Signal Hill, climbed from the car, and pulled Grace out by the hand.

"Come on, we're walking the rest of the way up."

"Now? In the dark?"

"Not dark, though, is it?" He did a half turn, his arm sweeping out, and she saw the joy in his eyes. "There's all this lovely moonlight."

"You're trying to weave a magic spell."

"I am. And this is the most magical place in St. John's. Come along with me, Mary Grace. Come look at the sea."

Her heart rose. Brendan always did this for her—lifted her, enchanted her. She found his company as irresistible as his kisses.

They climbed in silence, hand in hand, letting the enchantment grow till he said, "Do you remember the first time we came up here together?"

She did. In fact, she'd relived those moments a thousand times while they were apart. It had been the first time he told her he loved her.

"I remember every time we've been up here. But the first time wasn't at night."

"We stopped every twenty feet and did this." He paused and pulled her into his arms. The kiss, sweet and yearning, stopped her world from tilting and made everything right.

"Umm. A wonder we ever made it to the top."

"We were children then. Now I'm all grown up.

Took me a while."

He drew her on, and her breath came faster, but not all from the climb.

Cabot Tower, looking like a castle brooding in the moonlight, came into view at last, but he pulled her away from the parking lot, over to the shoulder of the headland, where the grass grew rough and wild. There they stood hand in hand and gazed out over the ocean.

Grace experienced a pang at the sheer beauty of it: wide water silvered by the moon, now nearly behind them on her way to set, and trailing her skirts in a bright train. Grace felt as if she hovered on the edge of the world, with only Brendan's fingers anchoring her—as if together the two of them could fly.

"Look out there, Mary Grace. Tell me what you see."

"Magic." The same she heard in his music.

"There is that. Want to know what I see? The future. Eternity. And I want to jump into it with you."

Keeping her fingers in his, he turned to face her. He drew a breath and dropped to one knee.

"Mary Grace Dawe, I love you. I never knew how much. My life's no good without you, so I'm willing to give it up into your hands if you'll take it. Will you be my wife?"

"Oh, Brendan. Oh, my God." Her free hand flew to her lips.

"Is that an answer? Oh, I nearly forgot."

He dug in his pocket and pulled out a small box. Grace's heart began to drum so hard she thought she might pass out.

Brendan flipped open the lid of the box and kissed the ring that lay inside. "This isn't worthy of you. I don't suppose there's a ring on earth that is. It's the best I could do. Can you see?"

She could. He turned the box and the clear moonlight illuminated what rested inside.

Oh, God, oh, God, oh, God. "It's beautiful."

"You sure?"

"I'm sure."

"I hope those are tears of happiness this time."

Grace, unaware she wept till he told her, mopped her face. She looked not at the ring but at the man she loved, kneeling at her feet.

For real this time.

"Mary Grace? An answer—please don't leave me hanging."

"Yes." What could she say but yes. "With one condition."

His eyes met hers. "Anything."

"Whatever decisions we make about our future we make together. That includes whether you give up your music."

"Agreed." Fumbling a bit, he plucked the ring from its box and slid it onto her finger.

"It fits."

"Of course it does. This is an enchanted night."

He kissed the ring again and turned her hand over to kiss the palm before he got to his feet.

There, on the edge of the world, she tumbled forward into his arms.

Chapter Twenty-Six

"I can hardly believe what a beautiful ring that is. Let me see it again," Darcy requested. "I just can't stop looking."

Neither could Grace. She'd already stolen a hundred glances at the rock on her hand, and it was barely ten a.m.

Darcy seemed almost as excited as Grace. "Look at that setting."

"Made in Ireland." Brendan had told her that on the way back down Signal Hill, his words interspersed with more kisses. "And there's a magic spell in Gaelic etched inside the band."

"What does it say?"

"That our union will be blessed with eternal love." Enduring as that shared by Charlie and Bridget? Grace wondered. No one had heard from Bridget on the subject.

Darcy sighed. "So romantic. It must have been the most romantic night of your life."

"Oh, yes." And she'd spent the balance of it in Brendan's arms, her dreams chased by the plaintive tones of fiddle music.

"Good thing you didn't set all those rumors straight, since they're true now. Have you set a date?"

"No, oh, no. Nothing like that yet."

"Yeah, I guess it's enough just to be engaged to

Brendan O'Rourke."

"We've some things to settle before we get married." Grace didn't want to focus on that.

"Do you think you'll have a big wedding?"

"No idea. Depends on what Brendan wants." Who'd have thought he'd prove such a romantic?

"Have you told your parents?"

"Not yet." Grace's parents had moved to Calgary to follow her father's work, back while Grace had been tramping the world. What would they say, knowing how Brendan had hurt her in the past? Whatever they thought—or said—she imagined they'd want to come home for the wedding.

Panic fluttered in her stomach. She'd think about that later. For now, what Darcy said was true: It was enough just being engaged to Brendan.

****

"What do you mean, no Europe? Have you lost your effing mind?"

Brendan had rarely seen Johnny Rideout so pissed. His brown eyes bugged nearly out of his head, and his complexion had gone all patchy like that of a man headed for a stroke. Brendan figured he was just too angry, though, to go down.

The two of them faced each other in the parlor on Garland Street, where Johnny and the other band members—plus Chrissy, of course—had once more turned up for practice, only to receive Brendan's news.

So far Rory and Ned had kept silent—not that Johnny, who'd immediately flown off the handle, gave them a chance to say anything.

"This is *Europe* we're talking about, O'Rourke— effing Europe! Our big chance."

"Everything's our big chance," Brendan said, unconsciously echoing Mary Grace. "That's what you said when we went dragging off to Chicago. Where's it end?"

"With effing fame, b'y! Isn't that what we've been chasing all this time? I can't believe you're standing there telling me this, now. You, of all people! Aren't you the one who effing broke us up because you said I was spending too much time with Chrissy?" Johnny gestured wildly. "Because I missed too many rehearsals? Because I didn't put the band first?"

"Yeah, but—"

"What the hell are you doing, eh?"

"Johnny," Chrissy put in.

Johnny rounded on her. "No, babe, I'm going to say my piece. He's got it coming, making me feel small for caring about you, for caring about anything but the music. And now that you and I have worked it out, now that you've stepped up to make sacrifices so we can be together, he's the one tossing it all to hell!"

Brendan looked from Johnny's furious eyes to Chrissy's distressed ones, then to Ned and Rory, both of whom seemed to weigh him carefully, waiting for what he'd say.

He drew a breath. "You're right, Johnny. It isn't fair, and I'm a right arsehole. Maybe I always was. Chrissy, I apologize for the way I treated you. It wasn't personal, and if you're willing to follow Johnny all around the world—well, he's a lucky man. But Mary Grace isn't willing to do that, and I need to put her first this time."

"Mary Grace!" Johnny exclaimed before anyone else could speak. "You've been crazy ever since the two of you got back together. I can't believe you'd get sucked in by a woman who'd ask you to give up the better part of yourself."

"Johnny," Chrissy cautioned again.

Brendan felt his own anger spark. "No, let him speak. We should all say what we think. Johnny, Mary Grace hasn't asked me to give anything up. This is me, making decisions."

"Damned stupid ones!"

"That's for you to think."

"Look…" Rory, ever reasonable, spoke for the first time. "There has to be room for compromise here. Johnny might be a pig-headed arse, but he compromised by coming here and trying to get the band back together. Chrissy and he both did—for the good of Kissin' the Cod. You telling me Grace won't do the same?"

"I'm telling you it has nothing to do with Mary Grace."

"Bullshit," Johnny snapped.

"Do you really want to bust us up again?" Ned asked. "Now, when we're poised to go up a notch?"

"I won't risk mucking up my relationship with Mary Grace. Not over this—not over anything."

"Listen to him!" Johnny flared. "But it was fine for him to ask me to 'put it on the back burner' with you, Chris. That was different."

"I've admitted I was a bastard over that."

"Maybe we could talk to Grace," Rory suggested. "Before you just jettison the band."

"Leave Mary Grace out of it," Brendan warned.

"I don't think we can," Ned objected. "Not if she's the reason you want to scuttle Europe."

"Europe," Johnny repeated. "That includes Dublin, in case you missed it. The old sod. What was it you always said about playing Ireland? Oh, yes—that you wanted to take the music back where it started. Just once. Isn't that what he said, b'ys?"

Sweating now, Brendan told his friends, "I'm not jettisoning the band. I'm willing to play here in St. John's. To record. But if you're off to Europe, then I suggest you find another fiddler."

A brittle silence fell, during which everyone stared at him with accusing eyes.

At last Ned spoke. "Another fiddler."

"I've given you plenty of notice. There must be a thousand fiddlers out there, all of them good. Brett can hook you up with someone—"

"Sure," Rory said in a dead tone, "there's a lot of fiddlers. A lot of good ones. None of 'em's Brendan O'Rourke."

"Band members change all the time."

"Not ours." Ned looked stricken. "Not us. You and Johnny started this band. You're the heart of it. You want to rip out the band's heart?"

"He already has, the two-faced bastard." Johnny shouted the words. "One way for me and Chrissy, another for him and his precious Mary Grace. Come on, b'ys, we can survive without him. Let's get the hell out of here."

"Johnny, wait," Chrissy said. "Don't be hotheaded. This is way too important."

"Yes," Rory put in. "Brendan, Grace managed without you for years. Do you really think one tour—"

"Don't beg him," Johnny spat at Rory. "It's over."

He gathered up his gear and, with Chrissy at his

heels, slammed out of the house. Neighbors all up and down Garland Street must have heard the reverberation.

Ned and Rory looked at each other. Slowly, Rory picked up his accordion case. "Johnny's wrong; it isn't over, Brendan. We can talk when everybody cools down."

Brendan shrugged. "Nothing to talk about. My decision's made."

"Well, damn," said Ned. "I guess I can see Johnny's point. Who says you get to make the decisions for all of us? And he's right, you know. You did ride him awful hard every time he took a minute for Chrissy. And she's carrying his kid."

"There have to be sacrifices," Rory said. "We all knew that going into it. How many promising relationships have I let slip by?"

"Talk to Grace," Ned urged. "She waited for you this long. Why not a bit longer?"

They left, far more quietly than Johnny.

"God damn it," Brendan said to himself. "I can't win."

"You have won, lad," Charlie materialized beside him, barely visible in daylight. "Sure, you've made the right choice at last, chosen the jewel of your heart."

"Then why do I feel like shit?"

Charlie grunted. "Ah, well—you're bound to feel that way, aren't you? Disappointing your friends like that. But they'll get over it, lad, and so will you. It isn't as if you have to give up the music entirely. You can still play down the pubs, at events. You can launch a solo career here in St. John's."

"That's so. I can."

"The main thing is you make Mary Grace happy as

I failed to do with my Bridget."

"You're right. Mary Grace's happiness is the main thing. The only thing."

Charlie beamed at him. "You've done well, lad. I'd slap you on the back if I could."

Chapter Twenty-Seven

"What's wrong, Mary Grace? Something's bothering you." Brendan hesitated before he added, "I thought you'd be happy with my decision."

They lay in the dark up in Brendan's room, having just shared the kind of lovemaking that turned a woman's bones to water. Grace took stock of herself with brutal honesty. She should be on top of the world, safe in the arms of the man she loved, in the city she loved, with nothing but happiness ahead of her. The promise of a wedding and a life together, endless nights just like this.

But she didn't feel too happy. Why?

She had everything she'd ever wanted. Brendan's promises, his devotion. His willingness to sacrifice for her.

Sacrifice.

That was it.

What had she told him? A relationship that rested on sacrifice couldn't survive.

Tears stung her eyes, and she blinked them back fiercely. She couldn't—wouldn't—weep over this, not when Brendan had done everything she'd asked, when he'd done all he could to make her happy, all the right things.

She couldn't do that to him.

He stroked her hair, and she felt the callouses on

the tips of his fingers—those put there by his devotion to his lifelong love of music. His other hand fidgeted with the stone of her diamond.

"You like your ring? Because we can exchange it if you'd prefer something else. Tommy said—"

"It's the most absolutely perfect ring. I wouldn't part with it for anything. You chose it for me, and I love it."

"Well then."

She felt his mind racing as he tried to figure out the source of her mood.

"If you're worried about Chet Hader—"

"I'm not."

"If it's the band—"

Bingo. The band.

She lay quiet, and his fingers stilled on hers.

"That's not your problem, Mary Grace."

"Of course it is. If it affects you, it affects me. I want you to be happy."

"I'm happy. I've never been so happy." He kissed her, a mark of devotion that had her eyes brimming with tears. "Trouble is, you're not, and I can't figure it."

"I'm happy. We're back together, and on some level I never stopped wanting that. I never stopped loving you."

"So?"

"So I know you, Brendan O'Rourke. Of all the things you are: funny, kind, smart, and talented, the *talented* comes first. Music's at your heart. If you were an onion and I peeled away all the layers, at the heart I'd find a nugget of pure music. I can't ask you to give that up."

"You haven't. I'm not giving up the music. Just—

just changing things a bit. Playing a different tune."

"But to give up the chance at Europe—" They'd discussed that earlier in the evening, over dinner. She still felt queasy.

"I don't need Europe." He drew her closer. "I have everything I need right here."

"The rest of the band—"

"I've been living for them, for the music, almost a decade. It's time for me—for us. Mary Grace, I tried living without you. It didn't work. And Charlie's shown me the cost of making bad choices. I won't go there again."

"You sound so sure."

"I am sure. Now you just concentrate on our future—what kind of wedding you want, where you'd like to live. We should probably start searching for a house." She felt him smile against her hair. "Preferably one without a ghost."

All her dreams—every one—held out to her on a silver platter. Then why couldn't she lose the ache inside?

****

"I hear you've broken up the band again. It's all over St. John's."

Brendan shot Barry a look from the corner of his eye. He'd stopped in at Fitzgerald's for a quick ale before meeting Mary Grace after work and bumped into his friend. At least, he thought gratefully, he hadn't run into any of his fellow band members. *Former* band members, he reminded himself.

Dryly, he said, "A few days ago, all anyone could talk about was my engagement to Mary Grace. Now it's the band."

"They're saying she's forced you to quit."

Brendan froze, his hand on his glass. "Who's saying that?"

"Everyone." Barry took a swig of ale. "People know why the two of you split way back when. They figure that's the price tag on her taking you back."

"Not true."

"Well you can't blame folks for thinking so, can you? You turn up complaining about Johnny and his girl—saying the band split over it. Next thing you're buying a rock the size of an iceberg and breaking Kissin' the Cod up all over again. It's a foregone conclusion, b'y."

Brendan swore with feeling. "By God. I just can't do anything right. Listen to me, Barry—you can tell anyone who asks I've finally got my priorities straight, putting people ahead of the music."

"Are you, though, old son? What about the people in the band—Johnny, Ned, and Rory?"

"I'm sorry about letting Ned and Rory down. Johnny can go stuff himself."

"What about the fans?" Barry went on, disregarding that. "Anyway, aren't you the one who always justified your devotion to the fiddle by saying it's more than just music? It's a living entity—like a person."

"Maybe I've learned better since then. I won't let anything get between me and Mary Grace this time."

Barry snorted. "Except your own stupidity."

Brendan took another gulp of ale and changed the subject. "How are things going with you and young Jenny?"

"Marvelously. Couldn't be better, in fact. I think I

may have met the love of my life."

"You have to be kidding." Brendan stared.

"I am not." Barry wiggled his eyebrows. "There's a lot to be said for a girl who can cook and keep her man satisfied, if you know what I mean." Barry leaned closer. "Those butter tarts, now. Mrs. Taylor's given her the recipe."

"Say no more." Brendan held up his hand. "I'll keep out of your love life, and you steer clear of mine."

****

So, Brendan thought some time later as he stood in the kitchen, staring out the window at the dark square of the yard filled with moonlight. If he'd done all he could to set his world right, if he'd proposed to Mary Grace and followed Charlie's advice, why was he still awake here on Garland Street?

At least Mary Grace slept, if restlessly. He'd left her upstairs and come down to the kitchen to do some thinking, try and sort out the misgivings keeping him from his rest. And, if he admitted it, hoping to encounter Charlie.

The kitchen, though, lay empty. And he wondered suddenly if the old man—his mission completed—had gone. Wouldn't that be a fine thing? Brendan could only celebrate the old boy being laid to rest at last, but he wouldn't mind using Charlie as a sounding board one more time.

Because he suspected he'd messed everything up—again. He didn't know how, when he'd tried so hard to make it all right. He'd done his best to rectify what he'd done wrong last time, to follow Charlie's advice, and make everybody as happy as possible. Trouble was nobody had ended up happy—except maybe Charlie.

Earlier he'd fielded a phone call from Chicago that had nearly blistered his ears. Brett Muskowitz had harangued him for half an hour about what a mistake he made by putting the band aside. Brett had talked about obligation and regret, putting all Brendan's own doubts in sharp relief.

Not that he had any real doubts—at least not about Mary Grace.

Brett had obviously heard from the other band members. He'd offered Brendan a limited tour to start—just the British Isles. The worst thing was that part of Brendan wanted to go.

They'd all had their separate dreams for the band. Rory's included reaching listeners with a reinvented, vital Celtic music. Ned's, a just payoff for all their hard work. Johnny wanted fame and money. Brendan...

Well, he'd always longed to play the pubs all around Britain and Ireland, where the music that lived inside him had been born.

"You're in a terrible stew, lad, for someone who has everything going his way." Charlie materialized beside him and rippled gently in the air.

"I am, and that's a fact." Brendan narrowed his eyes at the specter. "I thought you'd gone."

Charlie shook his head mournfully.

"I thought," Brendan persisted, "you'd maybe been laid to rest, now you've successfully reformed me."

"It seems I can't go to my rest until my lovely Bridget forgives me—or I have a proper wake, at least." Charlie scowled. "I don't see either of those things happening, do you?"

"Grand, just grand. I've barely had a full night's sleep since I got back to St. John's, and it looks like I won't, with you still underfoot."

Charlie drew himself up. "May I mention you're the one troubling me this time? What are you doing out of your warm bed?"

"That's what I'm asking myself."

Brendan toed out a kitchen chair, sat, and rested his head in his hands. "I just don't get it. I've done everything right, but no one's happy. The boys in the band—well, I didn't expect them to be happy. Or Brett Muskowitz. I'm letting them down."

"Unarguably so."

"But Mary Grace? You tell me why she's not happy! I've done everything she ever asked of me. I'm focusing on our relationship the way she always wanted."

"Lovely, lad!"

"I'm giving up Europe for her sake—I'm rocking my world to its foundations. So why do I see that look in her eyes? Why have I caught her crying half a dozen times—the woman I never saw cry even when we broke up?"

"Ah, well, women get emotional, don't they? They're creatures dominated by their feelings."

"Not Mary Grace. Anyway, she should be feeling pleased."

"She'll come 'round, lad. An awful lot has happened, and I'm sure she feels a wee bit bad about the band."

"I feel bad about the band." More than a wee bit.

"Yes, you've been together a long while. But it is a necessary evil, Brendan. You've said they'll find another fiddler, and they will."

Another fiddler. Brendan squirmed inwardly.

Another fiddler taking his place, driving the band he'd helped build from scratch, perhaps changing the very flavor of the music Kissin' the Cod produced. Ah, but that was no longer his business, was it? He had other fish to fry.

He needed to make Mary Grace happy, which would make him happy in turn, right?

"Charlie, tell me where I've gone wrong."

The ghost wavered in the air as if battered by Brendan's emotions.

"You've done everything right, lad. Give her time to find her feet. As for the music, is giving it up too steep a price to pay for seeing the light in her eyes?"

"No. But the light isn't there."

"It'll come, lad, it'll come."

A brief silence fell in the kitchen, which the ghost broke when he suggested, "Why don't you go off back to bed?"

"Because I'll just lie there unable to sleep. I can't stand it."

"Only one thing to do when you can't sleep, lad." Charlie nodded at his own fiddle case, abandoned on a chair in the corner. The case levitated, floated across the kitchen, and landed on the table at Brendan's elbow.

Like a man in a dream, Brendan took Guinevere from her case and began to play.

Chapter Twenty-Eight

The strains of fiddle music—soft and plaintive—wove through Grace's sleep, twined among her troubling dreams, and drew her toward wakefulness. The sound came from a distance, and it wept of loss and lamenting, of longing. Of love.

Breathless, Grace lay with her eyes wide in the dark bedroom. Without reaching out, she knew Brendan had left her. Somewhere he played his fiddle, for she recognized his touch on bow and strings, could now tell it from Charlie's, just as she knew it on her skin.

And what beauty he fashioned there in the night, diving and soaring through the quiet, whispering and singing enough to make a stone angel weep. As he always did, Brendan played what lay in his heart.

And he played grief. Sorrow. The last things she wanted him to feel.

She struggled up, naked beneath the sheet, and rested against the pillows, her ears straining. Sad as it was, she wanted to catch every note.

She knew the tune—loving Brendan, she would—"My Lagan Love." He rendered it with tender grace, intense emotion, and that hint of fire that characterized all his playing.

Filling the house, the music raised a chill on her arms and brought a lump to her throat.

Or maybe the chill came from the current of air

that stirred beside the bed, shimmered into light, and coalesced into the form of a woman.

Grace's breath, already stuck in her throat, threatened to choke her. She stared at the woman, who gazed back at her with calm eyes.

A ghost? Centuries of superstition roused in Grace's soul and told her so. She could both see the woman's form and see through it—the dresser and part of the closet door behind.

Not so tall as Grace and slender as a willow, the woman wore her hair in a loose knot at the back of her head and had a sweet, oval face. The eyes—her best feature—regarded Grace seriously from beneath level brows.

For a dozen of Grace's heartbeats, they stared at one another before Grace managed to fight for words. "Bridget O'Rourke?" she croaked out.

The ghost nodded. Grace's heart raced wildly in her chest. Brendan had said nothing about Bridget making an appearance. Had she been here all the while? But Charlie told Brendan his wife had moved on beyond her husband's reach.

What to do? Should Grace flee the room? Run downstairs, call Brendan?

Bridget tipped her head as if listening. "Hark to that, now." She spoke with a lilting accent. "He plays almost as well as my Charlie, does that Brendan." She smiled and her face lit, filling with youth and beauty. "The talent breeds true in these O'Rourke men."

"It does." As unobtrusively as possible, Grace slid to the edge of the bed away from the pale figure.

"You've no need to fear me, Mary Grace Dawe."

"No?"

"Why should I wish to hurt you, or anyone? I spent my life looking after my own and doing my best to harm none. But your emotions are all in turmoil. I could feel them through the ether."

"Oh? I'm sorry if I disturbed you."

"Not that. I often drop by to listen to Charlie when he plays."

"Does he know you're here?"

"No, my dear, he can't sense me—his grief won't let him. Tell me, Mary Grace Dawe: When you listen to your man play his music, what do you hear?"

Grace drew another difficult breath. "Beauty. Fire. So much talent…"

"All those things, yes. There's more."

"Yes? Tell me."

To Grace's surprise, the ghost perched on the other side of the bed, though the mattress didn't dip.

"It's what I came to tell you, when I sensed your emotions. It isn't easy loving a man such as Charlie or Brendan. You do love him?"

"Oh, yes."

"I loved my Charlie, too. But I failed him."

"*You* failed *him*? That's not the way Brendan tells it."

"Ah, well, but Brendan's heard only Charlie's side. It took me all these years—seventy of them since Charlie died—to understand what I couldn't see at the time. I was so unfair to him."

Grace's stomach clenched. "I've been feeling that way too."

"You can't love a man for what he is and then turn around and ask him to be something else. These O'Rourke men…" The ghost shook her head. "If

Brendan's like Charlie, the music isn't just music—it's breath and blood. Playing isn't just playing—it's the language of his heart. That beautiful song your man is playing for you—do you know what that is? It's his love for you."

Grace's fingers tightened on the sheet, her eyes filled with tears. All the emotions she'd been feeling for days came together into a single thought.

"Oh," she gasped. "Oh, my God, you're right. Why didn't I see?"

"Not easy to see, my dear—especially when a woman's blinded by her own needs and impatience and the demands on her. I kept thinking, 'Why can't that Charlie just snap into shape, stop the shenanigans, get a steady job instead of spending his nights in the boozers drinking and playing that blessed music?' I never saw the truth until it was much, much too late. The music made him the charming, maddening, wonderful man he was. If he'd given it up, he just wouldn't have been Charlie O'Rourke."

"But he left you to raise a child on your own, right? To struggle on for years."

This time Bridget's smile looked sad. "That's why I'm here, lass. The span of our lives is not set; we never know how long we have. Do not waste it being at odds with your man. And take his love however he can give it—even if that's in a beautiful song. There's no room for sacrifice on either side, understand?"

"I do." It had been the one truth insistently gnawing at Grace for days. "Thank you."

Bridget arose. "Well, I've said my piece, and I expect you know what to do. Time for me to go."

"Wait." Grace reached out to the ghost. "There

must be a way for you to let Charlie know you're here and that you still love him. You do still love him?"

"I never stopped. How could I fail to love a man with that much beauty inside him?"

How, indeed?

"Then you need to tell him and end his misery."

Bridget smiled again. "The way you're going to tell Brendan he doesn't need to make sacrifices to keep your love?"

"Yes."

"Lass, you haven't been listening. I can't make Charlie hear me. Don't you think I've tried, these many years? I long to take him away with me to everlasting bliss. He's rooted here, held by his own guilt and pain."

"How can he break his bonds? What can free him so he can see you?"

"I can't say. He needs to forgive himself before he'll hear my voice. That's all I know."

"There must be a way to free him."

"If you can do that, lass, I'll be waiting. Just as I have this long, long while."

With that, Bridget transformed into a bright wisp of ether, twined through the air of the bedroom, and dissipated like so much fog.

Chapter Twenty-Nine

Brendan lowered his bow when Mary Grace entered the kitchen, where he sat with his heels propped on a chair and Guinevere tucked under his chin. She wore nothing but his shirt, and her hair flowed loose over her shoulders. His heart stuttered in his chest just as it did every time he saw her—and always would.

"I'm sorry, did I wake you? I should have thought. I just needed to do some thinking." He gestured with the bow. "The music helps."

"You didn't disturb me—it sounded beautiful. Plaintive. And very sad." She edged out a chair and slid into it, facing him. "Brendan, we need to talk."

His heart dropped. Carefully, he set Guinevere and the bow on the table and drew a breath. "Are you breaking up with me? I wondered if it was coming. You're not happy, right? I could feel that."

"I'm not breaking up with you."

"Then what's going on? You're not acting like a woman who's happy—or in love."

She studied him gravely. "If I'm unhappy, Brendan, it's because you are."

"Me? I've never been so happy. Finally got my head straight and made the right choices. At least, I thought I had."

"Then why are you sitting down here in the middle of the night playing music sad enough to make me weep?"

"I can't sleep in this house. And I told you, I needed to think."

"About what?"

"About how I can make you happy, Mary Grace. About keeping from making the mistakes Charlie did."

"I see. Well, if you ask me, Charlie's still giving you bad advice."

"About putting you first?" Brendan frowned. "How can that be?"

"Putting me first is fine; it's putting you last that has me worried. Brendan, it won't work. It can't."

"Why?"

"Because you can't deny the man you are inside." She reached out and touched Guinevere's strings. "Not for long, anyway. After a while, even with the best of intentions, bitterness will set in. That's the trouble with sacrifice."

He searched her eyes in the dim light. "What's brought all this on?"

Mary Grace smiled wryly. "I had a visitor upstairs. She came to listen to your music. She listens to Charlie, too, though he can't tell she's there. And she loves him; she still does after all this time."

"Bridget? You're telling me Bridget O'Rourke appeared to you?"

"I am."

"Well, I'll be damned. What did she say?"

"She told me I can't claim to love you and yet expect you to turn into someone else. That—as she pointed out—was the mistake she made. If I love you, I have to love all of you, from the beauty in your heart to your propensity to leave up the toilet seat—"

"She mentioned that, did she?"

"No, I put that in—to your need to tour Europe." Mary Grace leaned across the table and kissed him, a gesture sweet with devotion. "And I do love you, Brendan O'Rourke."

"My God, Mary Grace." His heart pounded.

"And that means I accept you. I accept that your love is mine but that music has a strong—and rightful—claim on you also. And if the music calls you to go away from me for a while, my heart will just have to expand enough to accept that."

He pushed the fiddle aside and clasped both her hands in his tenderly. "Just what are you saying?"

"That I want to be Brendan O'Rourke's wife, and I understand who he is—a musician. That I trust our love to endure even if we're apart a few weeks at a time. That I'd rather share you with the music than sentence you to a life without it. I love you that much." Mary Grace gulped. "I love the man you are, the man you've always been."

"Mary Grace." A wave of emotion surged through him, equal parts joy, humility, and shattering relief. "Are you sure about this? I mean, an appearance by a ghost has become commonplace around here. And you're saying my spook didn't offer the best advice."

"Bridget told me nothing I didn't already know. I just couldn't put it into words. And yes, I'm sure. Call the boys; tell them you're up for the tour, if you want to go. If you don't—that's fine with me too. But if you go, I'll be waiting for you when you come home."

Brendan closed his eyes for a moment, feeling the truth of her emotions, of her love. When he opened them again, she gave him a wobbly smile. "As I say, what's a few weeks compared with seventy years?"

He raised her hands to his lips and kissed them one after the other.

"If I want to go," he repeated. "If I can bear being away from you that long... Maybe I can talk the boys into that limited schedule. I'd love to play Dublin. And, you know, you could come with me."

"I could, if I find someone to cover at the museum. Maybe I'll go with you on the next tour, or the one after that. For now—" Her eyes, full of love and belief, met his. "I think you need to fly, and I need to learn to trust that the ties between us will bring you back again."

"So long as you believe they will, and remember that every song I play is for you." He drew her closer across the table and kissed her again. "My love will always bring me home; that ring you wear assures it."

"I know. So now do you think we can go back upstairs and get some sleep?"

Brendan thought about it. A new peace filled him, one for which it seemed he'd been reaching far too long. Just one problem remained...

"What about Charlie? I hate to leave him dangling, after he went out of his way to try and help me. Surely Bridget hinted at some way to reunite them?"

Mary Grace shook her head. "She said it's his own guilt and unhappiness keeping him from seeing her. He's the one doubting their bond."

"Yes, and he's earned that guilt. He abandoned her to a hard life for selfish reasons. I know how I'd feel."

"The real sticking point, as I see it, is he doesn't feel worthy of Bridget's love. How can we change how he feels about himself?"

A light went on in Brendan's mind. A smile

crossed his face and he snapped his fingers.

"I think I might just know. I've been awake here on Garland Street ever since I got home." His eyes danced. "Maybe it's time for a wake on Garland Street."

Chapter Thirty

The house on Garland Street fairly burst with people. They crammed the kitchen—leaving only a small cleared space around the table where sat the members of Kissin' the Cod—packed the parlor, and spilled out through the open door into the street. Drink flowed liberally, the very best Irish whiskey and the infamous Newfoundland rum. Anticipation sizzled in the air. Folks had left work early and waited with bated breath for the sun to sink and the beautiful northern light to fade.

Brendan eyed his fellow musicians. Johnny sat beside him, his guitar balanced on his knee and Chrissy at his back, a serene look in his brown eyes. That worried Brendan a little bit; he couldn't remember the last time Johnny had looked so content.

Rory and Ned, both with their instruments at the ready, looked joyful as little boys on the last day of school. They'd accepted the news that Brendan would be accompanying them on tour with astonished gratitude. They'd all agreed on a limited schedule to the British Isles for this first leg, and used a conference call to inform Brett, together.

"The fame will come when it comes," Rory had articulated. "It's the music—and loving it—that counts."

And Brendan had overheard Chrissy say to Mary

Grace, "I'm glad the band has decided to stay based in St. John's—I adore this city. And I'm relieved they've shortened up the tour. With a baby coming, Johnny's going to have to adjust his priorities, too."

Convincing the band—and the city of St. John's—to hold a wake for a fellow seventy years dead had proved more of a challenge. Johnny thought Brendan had gone crazy, and couldn't justify the cost of the casket now lying in the parlor. The fact that the casket, around which so many people currently congregated, held ice and liquor mollified him a bit.

"His Bridget couldn't afford a fine coffin," Brendan declared, "and I'm doing it up right."

"Honoring the man—a fellow musician," put in Rory, who'd seemed to embrace it right away.

Ned, tossing back a drink, had agreed. "It's just what I'd want other musicians to do for me."

Johnny could only agree. "Yes, well, what the hell, eh, b'ys?"

Now Brendan exchanged a look with Mary Grace in her place by the sink. He could feel her anticipation and see the love in her eyes—enough to allow him to be *him*, enough to trust they would always be reunited.

Just like Charlie and Bridget? He could only hope so.

When the house went quiet—a hush that seemed to spread out into the street—and the light softened outside the windows, he could wait no longer. He raised Guinevere, tucked her under his chin, and gave a short laugh.

"Let's do this."

He lit into the "March of the King of Laois," pouring himself into it, playing with fire. His bow danced across the strings, and he struck a sharp rhythm, letting the music take hold of him, become part of him. The world held its breath as he went once through the tune. Then Johnny joined in, his fingers nimble on the guitar strings, his foot tapping unconsciously under the table. Sparks flew from Brendan's bow.

With a smile, Rory brought his accordion in on the third round. Someone in the parlor, unable to control his exuberance, hooted. When Ned joined with the bodhran, swelling the sound still further and giving it a heartbeat, folks began to clap in time. The house on Garland Street rocked, and the music spilled out into the city, down into the harbor, and to eternity.

Would it be enough? Would Charlie understand he was being honored at last? That he deserved to be celebrated, was worthy of his Bridget's love?

Would she come for him? Would he see her—see her love, strong and constant, at last—when she did?

Brendan blinked tears from his eyes and found Mary Grace's face across the kitchen. Because of her, he knew the love had no end.

People in the kitchen—and outside, for all Brendan knew—were dancing. The music pounded on, led by Guinevere's searing notes, until all at once Brendan caught the faint strains of another fiddle accompanying his own—notes twining through his, complimenting and harmonizing with faultless speed and precision. Glancing up, he saw Charlie standing at Mary Grace's side, elbows akimbo as he fiddled fiercely, euphoria filling his countenance.

Brendan fiddled still faster, a grin breaking over his face. The band, as if connected with him telepathically, kept up as the pace increased impossibly, fueled by sheer talent rather than intention.

At the height of it, Brendan caught his breath in wonder as another pale shape took form in the kitchen. He told Charlie, speaking the words in his mind, "She's come for you, old man. You can trust the music to us. It's time to go home."

Charlie stopped playing his spectral fiddle. Was Brendan the only one who heard that thread of music cease? Charlie turned and saw the slender shade that stood just beside him. His face transformed with joy, and the fiddle in his hand dissipated like so much smoke. Bridget moved into his arms as he gathered her to his heart.

One moment they trembled there together, lips fused. The next they had gone, and Brendan ended the tune with a flourish. Just the first tune of many this night. No one would be getting any sleep on Garland Street.

****

"Did you see them?" Brendan's eyes looked a bit wild. Grace could tell energy still poured through him even though it was now after six in the morning and all the guests had gone. St. John's embraced a new day. "Did you? They kissed, and he went away with her."

Grace shook her head. The only thing she'd seen last night was the man she loved in his element, fire flying from his fingertips and sheer joy in his eyes. How grateful she felt that she hadn't taken that from him!

"I didn't see, but I believe you."

"The house feels different, doesn't it?" He cocked his head. "I believe he's gone."

"I'm glad. He's at peace, and she doesn't have to

wait any longer for him." Grace pressed forward into Brendan's arms and gazed into his eyes. "Waiting is hard. But sometimes it's worth it."

"Do you know how much I love you, Mary Grace Dawe?"

"Yes. I can hear it every time you play a note."

"Amen." He drew her closer. "Tour's set for September. Sure you won't come with me?"

She shook her head regretfully. "Not this time. There'll be plenty other tours."

"Then let's get married before I go—a small, private ceremony. Or anything else you want."

She lifted an eyebrow. "Small sounds nice—I don't know if you'll get away with private in this town."

"You're saying you will?"

"I'm saying the wedding's a formality. I've belonged to you since the first time you smiled at me, Brendan O'Rourke."

He gave her a long kiss, passionate as his music. "I guess this means you trust me."

"It does." She smiled crookedly. "Even more, I suspect it means I've learned to trust myself."

The second kiss curled her toes and made her forget everything else.

She whispered, "The party's done, the ice in the casket's melted—I don't know what your mother will say about her floor—and the house is empty. Come upstairs with me?"

"Gladly, though I'm still pretty pumped. I'm not sure I'll be able to sleep."

"Oh, Brendan, love of my life, I was hoping you'd say that."

A word about the author...

Born and raised in Western New York, Laura Strickland has pursued lifelong interests in lore, legend, magic and music, all reflected in her writing. She has made pilgrimages to both Newfoundland and Scotland in the company of her daughter, but is usually happiest at home not far from Lake Ontario, with her husband and her "fur" child, a rescue dog.

Author of Scottish romances *Devil Black*, *His Wicked Highland Ways*, *Honor Bound: A Highland Adventure* and *The Hiring Fair* as well as The Guardians of Sherwood Trilogy consisting of *Daughter of Sherwood*, *Champion of Sherwood* and *Lord of Sherwood*, she has also published three Steampunk romances, *Dead Handsome: a Buffalo Steampunk Adventure*, *Off Kilter: a Buffalo Steampunk Adventure* and *Sheer Madness: a Buffalo Steampunk Adventure* and two Christmas novellas—*The Tenth Suitor* and *Mrs. Claus and the Viking Ship*—and a Valentine's novella: *Ask Me*. Her Lobster Cove Historical Romances include *The White Gull* and the novella *Forged By Love*, soon to be followed by a sequel, *Words and Dreams*. *Awake on Garland Street* is her sixteenth book with The Wild Rose Press.